THE ONLY BOO

. . . what you<del>r</del> days of rain (p. 243)

. . . where PMS is mentioned in the Bible (p. 11)

. . . proof that Jimi Hendrix slept with Liberace (p. 101)

. . . about the new divorced Barbie doll (p. 78)

. . . why the woman's toes were curling when she made love (p. 120)

. . . the difference between a lawyer and a sperm cell (p. 143)

. . . how to make God laugh (p. 56)

. . . and hundreds more jokes, stories, riddles, and one-liners!

NEW YORK CITY CAB DRIVER'S JOKE BOOK, VOL. 2— IT'S A HAIL OF A READ!

ALSO BY JIM PIETSCH

The New York City Cab Driver's Joke Book

The
NEW YORK CITY
CAB DRIVER'S
JOKE
BOOK

VOLUME 2

WRITTEN AND ILLUSTRATED BY

Jim Pietsch

WARNER BOOKS

NEW YORK   BOSTON

WARNER BOOKS EDITION

Cover design and illustration by Jon Valk

Visit our Web site at
www.warnerbooks.com

Warner Books, Inc.
1271 Avenue of the Americas
New York, NY 10020

 A Time Warner Company

Printed in the United States of America

First Printing: April, 1998

10 9 8 7 6

*This book is dedicated to
all the joke tellers
who keep laughter circulating
around the world*

Acknowledgments

I must thank Dave Goldstein of Warner Books for suggesting to me that I write a second volume of *The New York City Cab Driver's Joke Book*. His encouragement was the inspiration that started this crazy ball rolling.

This book would also have been impossible for me to write without all the great joke tellers that have come to my joke parties. Their participation has contributed an endless supply of hilarity to these gatherings, and many of the jokes in this book are here because of the generosity and senses of humor shared with me by these wonderful people. A special mention must go to Larry Bassen, whose joke telling is well on its way to becoming legendary.

I would also like to express my thanks to two of my favorite joke tellers of all time: Willa Bassen and John "Ethan" Phillips. Not only have they provided me with countless great jokes over the years, but they also took the time to read through this manuscript. Their comments were invaluable to me during the final editing phase of this book.

A thank-you also goes to my editor at Warner Books, Rob McMahon. His patience, understanding, and comedic insight has helped to make this collection a much stronger presentation.

I must also thank my ever-widening circle of joke tellers and friends, whose laughter and love are truly what keep me going: Frank and Christine Baier, Donald Burton, Dalia Carella, Chris Cohen, Didi Conn, Mary Clare Ditton, Jim Donaldson and Julie Marable, Danny Epstein, Mary Fahl, Ann Faldermeyer, Eric Frandsen, Jeff Ganz, Jennifer Gaspari, Laurie Gehen, J.R. Goetcheus, Peggy Gordon, Doug Hall, Steve Holtzer, Selma Lewis, B.J. Liederman, Paul Lovelace, Roy Miller, Gary Moscato, Jeff Nelson, George Paris, Allan Pepper, The Pride family, Joanne Regan, Eddie "Gua Gua" and the Rivera family, Ginny Roberts, Hillary Rollins, Jeremy Ross, Joe Scibana, Keith Shapiro, Marty Sheller, Georg Wadenius, Tom Werts, Bob Waldman, Patrik Williams, Karl Woitach, Mark Worthy, Jay and Denise Yerkes, and Christoph Zuppinger.

Much love and thanks, of course, to my family: Drs. William and Weezie Pietsch, Barbara and Berk Adams, Patti Pietsch-Wise, and Mark, Shauna, and Alea Wise.

And, as always, my heartfelt gratitude goes to my good friend Patti Breitman.

Introduction

*O*n that wintry evening in 1985, as I was driving south on Broadway, I decided to veer off onto West End Avenue to look for a fare. At the corner of 102nd Street, a woman hailed me and I pulled over. When she got into my cab, I had no idea that this woman would change my life.

Quite a number of different circumstances had converged on this particular night to put me in that proverbial "right place at the right time."

I was a musician, trying to survive the struggle of the artistic existence in New York City. Having been a joke lover and joke teller all my life, when I began driving a cab in 1984 I hoped that one of the fringe benefits of the job would be that I would hear all the best jokes in the world. I found this to be true, but to a degree that went far beyond my wildest dreams.

I asked the question, "Heard any good jokes lately?" to nearly everyone that got into my taxi. I was surprised to find that nine out of ten people would say, "I can't remember jokes." Fortunately, the other ten percent of my passengers were people like me: Jokesters who love hearing and telling good anecdotes and one-liners.

I started hearing more great jokes than I ever thought possible. I heard clean jokes from dirty old men and dirty jokes from beautiful young women. I traded jokes with blue-collar workers, intellectuals, and world famous celebrities.

I bought a little notebook and started keeping a record of all the great jokes that were told to me. At stop lights and in traffic jams, I would jot down a few words about the latest jokes I had heard, and throughout the day I would tell these jokes to my passengers, thereby cementing them in my brain.

Through all of this, I began to discover the true power of jokes. I can now fully understand why they always say that you should "open with a joke." Once you have shared a laugh with someone you have made a connection, and on some level you feel like you have become friends.

From starting out sharing jokes with people in the back seat of my taxi, I would often get into very interesting discussions with them about what kind of work they did. I discovered a great deal about life in general, and about New York in particular. I learned about many different jobs and lifestyles here that I never before knew existed. I found out that New York City is a place where not only anything *can* happen, it's a place where it usually *does*.

Which leads me back to 102nd Street and West End Avenue. After the woman told me her destination, I was trying to decide whether to ask her the usual question, "Heard any good jokes lately?" I was beginning to feel tired and since women don't usually tell jokes, I thought that her answer would probably be, "No, have you?"

I wasn't sure that I had the energy at that moment to start telling some jokes, but on the spur of the moment, I decided to take a chance and I asked her the question. I got a sudden jolt of energy when she gave me the best answer I had ever gotten. She said, "You go first!"

We started trading jokes with each other, and she told me some really funny ones. We were taking turns cracking each other up, and luckily I had just had a joke party the night before, so I had a gazzillion great new ones. After a while she just said, "Go ahead, you keep telling them. I'm usually the one telling all the jokes, and it's so refreshing to have someone telling them to *me* for a change."

We got to her destination, and while she was getting the money out of her purse for the fare, she said to me with a smile, "You know so many great jokes, you should write a book."

I said, "I'm going to." I showed her my little book of joke notes and said, "I've been writing them down for six months with that exact purpose in mind."

The woman then told me, "I'm an editor for Warner Books. Here is my business card."

Two weeks later I took a proposal up to her at her office. She called me back the next day with an offer, and *The New York City Cab Driver's Joke Book* was born.

That was over ten years ago, and that book spun

my life off in a completely different direction than what I had ever expected. The cartoons in the book led to my doing a comic strip for the newspapers *Taxi Talk* in New York and the *Toronto Taxi News*. The comic strip led to a job for several years as a graphic artist. I also co-produced, was music director, and co-wrote the story for an hour-long comedy video based on the *Cab Driver's Joke Book*. It was during this project that I got into a video editing room for the first time, and I fell in love with the process. I am now a professional video editor and work in the television industry.

Changing careers is not financially profitable on an immediate basis, so I continued to drive a cab, but the number of days that I drove each year became fewer and fewer. I did not, however, hear correspondingly fewer and fewer jokes. You see, after my book was published I became a joke magnet.

People who know me are always telling me jokes and trying to stump me on one that I haven't already heard. Every year or so I have a party where I get all my best joke telling friends together, and the fun and laughter goes on for hours. I now have a very large network of joke tellers and whenever we hear a new joke, we call each other up on the telephone. We all hope to be the first on our block to tell the new one going around town. For some reason, I usually seem to be at the hub of this ever-expanding wheel. A friend of mine eventually dubbed me "The Johnny Appleseed of Jokes."

So the jokes in this book have come from many different sources, as well as from the back seat of my taxi. The main thing that the jokes have in common is that they are truly funny. In compiling this volume, I was extremely pleased when I realized how many great new jokes I have heard since my first book was published.

After all these years of sharing and trading anecdotes and one-liners, people occasionally ask me if I ever get tired of jokes. It's actually just the opposite. Jokes are a great source of fun, and I am fully convinced that frequent laughter is one of the most essential ingredients to a happy, fulfilled life.

One of the things that I love most about jokes is that *anyone* can tell them. You don't have to be a comedian to be able to get laughs from your friends and business associates. A wide variety of people from all different walks of life are *fantastic* joke tellers.

Even though ninety percent of the people I asked for jokes in my taxi said that they couldn't remember them, at least fifty percent of those people told me that they *knew* a great joke teller. "Oh, I wish my brother was here, he's got a million of them," they would say. Or, "There's this guy I work with who's amazing. Each day he comes in with a new joke."

So jokes are for everyone, and I am really happy to present you with this new collection. As in my first book, I want to remind you that I do not necessarily agree with the viewpoints expressed in these jokes.

Some of the them may be of questionable taste and political incorrectness, but these are the jokes that are floating around and making a lot of people laugh.

I must also apologize for any show biz jokes that are too inside for people who aren't in "the business." Since so many years of my life have been spent in the entertainment industry, these jokes hold a special place in my heart. Also, in this book I have once again included some true-life cab driving stories, *and these are in italics.*

I truly love the work I do now as a video editor, but sometimes I miss being in the gold mine of jokes on the streets of Manhattan. I know that the jokes are still rolling around out there, but I'm not. It was a wonderful experience to have such a diverse array of people telling me their favorite jokes, and to have them laughing at mine.

I calculated that while driving a cab I asked approximately 40,000 people the question, "Have you heard any good jokes lately?" They were kind enough to share them with me, and I feel blessed to once again have the opportunity of sharing them with you.

The phenomenon of jokes is truly remarkable. No one knows where they come from, and yet new ones keep surfacing all the time. They are transmitted from one person to another with no purpose in mind other than to bring a momentary burst of joy. For me, in my life, I can't think of any better way to spend my energy.

If you happen to find some new favorites in this book, please go out and tell them to anyone and everyone you choose. Feel free to recklessly and indiscriminately scatter chuckles and guffaws here, there, and everywhere. A little joviality can truly go a long way. Much further, I must admit, than I ever expected.

A surgeon, an architect, and an economist are having a discussion, and they begin to argue about whose profession is the oldest.

The surgeon condescendingly says to the other two men, "Well, you know that God took a rib out of Adam to make Eve, so I think that it is rather obvious that surgery is the oldest profession."

"Ah," says the architect, "but before that, out of total chaos, God made the heavens and the earth. So I think it's quite obvious that architecture is the oldest profession."

The economist merely folds his arms and smiles serenely. "And where," he asks, "do you think the total chaos came from?"

Last night I slept like an attorney. First I'd lie on one side, then I'd lie on the other.

A woman goes into a bar with a little Chihuahua dog on a leash. She sits down at the bar next to a drunk. The drunk rolls around, leans over, and *splat!* He pukes all over the dog. The drunk looks down, sees the little dog struggling in the pool of vomit, and slurs, "I don't remember eating *that!*"

Q: What's the difference between a savings bond and a man?
A: A savings bond matures.

And the show biz variation:

Q: What's the difference between a savings bond and a musician?
A: Eventually, a savings bond matures *and makes money*.

God tells Adam that he has decided to give him a companion called a woman. Adam says, "A woman? What's that?"

God explains, "She will be beautiful beyond your wildest dreams. She will wait on you hand and foot. She will be your most trustworthy friend, a fantastic lover, and a brilliant conversationalist. She will be a gourmet cook, a wonderful homemaker, and will bear you well-behaved, thoughtful children who will always get along with one another. And finally, she will, of course, laugh at all your jokes."

"Wow!" says Adam. "That sounds great! How are you going to make this woman?"

God replies, "I'm going to make her out of one of your legs."

"Hmm," says Adam. "What could I get for a rib?"

A man says to his wife, "You never tell me when you have an orgasm."

The wife replies, "You're never home."

A woman walks into a tattoo parlor. She goes up to the tattoo artist and says, "I love boxing and I think it's the greatest sport ever. I watch it all the time, read all about it, and I want you to do a job for me."

"Sure," says the tattoo artist. "What would you like?"

The woman explains, "I want two tattoos, one on each thigh. On my right thigh, I want a portrait of Muhammad Ali; on my left thigh, a portrait of Mike Tyson. They are my two favorite boxers of all time."

"Well," says the artist, somewhat hesitantly, "that's a pretty big job. That'll be expensive."

"Money is no object," replies the woman. "Just give me something to knock me out while you do the job."

"All right," agrees the tattoo artist. He hands the woman a bottle, and she drinks it until she passes out.

The artist starts the tattoos, and he quickly gets completely absorbed in his work, losing all track of time. Six hours later, he leans back to view his handiwork, and he realizes that this is his masterpiece.

He is extremely proud, and he excitedly wakes up the woman. "Look! Look!" he says. The woman slowly regains consciousness, and is still a little groggy when she looks down at her thighs. "What's this?" she asks.

"What do you mean, 'What's this?'" says the shocked tattoo artist. "It's the two tattoos you wanted!"

"But—but . . ." stammers the woman. "It doesn't look *anything* like them."

"Are you kidding?" says the incredulous tattoo artist. "It looks *exactly* like them!"

"No, it doesn't," says the woman. She motions back and forth between her thighs and whines, "Can't even tell which one is supposed to be which!"

"It's Ali on the *right*, Tyson on the *left*, just like you wanted," exclaims the tattoo artist.

"This is terrible!" cries the woman. "Now I have to live with this for the rest of my life!"

She gets up and starts to leave, but the tattoo artist stops her. "Wait a minute, lady," he says. "I did a lot of work for you. You owe me some money."

At this, the woman becomes furious. "I'm not paying for this! You did a lousy job!"

"I did *not*!" shouts the tattoo artist. "I did a *great* job. It looks *just* like them."

"No, it doesn't!" yells the woman, and she bursts out of the tattoo parlor.

The man chases her out onto the street, and just

then a bum happens to be walking by. The tattoo artist runs up to the woman, pulls up her dress, points down, and shouts to the bum, "Who are these boxing greats?"

The bum staggers a moment, then drunkenly slurs, "I'm not sure about the guy on the right. The guy on the left . . . I don't know. But the guy in the middle is *definitely* Don King!"

■▼■

Q: Did you hear about the new Jewish-American Princess horror movie?
A: It's called *Debbie Does Dishes*.

Q: Did you hear about the new Jewish-American Princess porno movie?
A: It's called *Debbie Does Nothing*.

■▼■

Very late one night, I picked up a man outside the Plaza hotel. When I asked him what kind of work he did, he told me that he was the bartender there. He told me that one night many years ago, Jackie Gleason had come into the hotel bar with a number of friends. Early in the evening, Mr. Gleason said to this bartender, "So tell me, what's the biggest tip you ever got?"

The bartender replied, "A hundred dollars, Mr. Gleason."

"Well, tonight," Jackie said, "I'm going to give you a hundred and fifty."

Many hours later, when Gleason was settling up his bill, he walked over to the bartender and, true to his word, gave him a hundred-and-fifty-dollar tip. "So tell me," Jackie said, feeling pretty self-satisfied after he had handed the huge tip to the bartender, "who was it that gave you the hundred dollar tip?"

The bartender replied, "It was you, Mr. Gleason."

Jackie just threw his head back and laughed.

■▼■

A suspected foreign terrorist arrives at Kennedy Airport and is going through customs. He becomes extremely irate when the customs inspector insists on searching his bags. He screams at the inspector, "New York is the asshole of the world!"

"And I take it," replies the inspector, "that you're just passing through."

■▼■

Two middle-aged Jewish men are talking. One says to the other, "You know, last weekend I had a *good* Shabbus."

"I'm glad to hear it," his friend replies. "It's always nice when you can have a good day on the Holy Sabbath. What did you do?"

"Well," says the first man, "on Friday evening, all of my grown children came home and spent the night. Saturday morning we all got up, put on our finest clothes, and went to temple. It was a very beautiful, moving service. Then we came back to the house, had bagels and lox, and shared family stories. Then I rented the movie *The Ten Commandments* and we all sat down as a family and watched it together. Then my wife cooked a fantastic dinner. It was a *good* Shabbus."

"As a matter of fact," says the other man, "last weekend I had a good Shabbus too."

"You don't say?" replies the first man. "What did you do?"

"Early Saturday morning," says the other man, "a friend of mine and I went to a bar and got rip-roaring drunk. Then we went to a brothel and got ourselves a couple of hookers. We took them to a cheap, sleazy hotel, where I screwed one and my friend screwed the other. Then we did a switch. I did his and he did mine. Then I went home and screwed my wife until I fell asleep. It was a *good* Shabbus."

"How can you call that a *good* Shabbus?" says the first man, staring at his friend in shocked disbelief. "That's a *great* Shabbus!"

Q: What's the difference between boogers and broccoli?
A: Kids won't eat broccoli.

One balmy evening in Rome the Pope decides to take a walk. He slips out the rear door of the Vatican and is walking through the back alleys of Rome when he sees a ten-year-old boy smoking a cigarette. The Pope gently says to him, "Young man, you're much too young to smoke!"

The kid looks up at the Pope and says, "Fuck you!"

The Pope is completely taken aback. "What?" he says. "You say that to *me*, the Pontiff, the Vicar of Christ, the head of the entire Roman Catholic Church? I am the spiritual leader for millions of people, young man, the representative of God, and you dare say that to *me*? No, no, no, kid. FUCK *YOU*!"

■▪▪

Q: What's the best thing to throw to a drowning guitar player?
A: His amplifier.

■▪▪

A guy goes to the doctor and tells him that he keeps having these loud farts that don't smell. "They're really gigantic, Doc," the man says, "and it's really embarrassing. I mean, sometimes I'll be making love to a woman and suddenly, out of nowhere, I'll let out this humongous fart. Fortunately, as I said, they don't *smell*, but they're just so loud that I'm totally mortified."

"Does this happen any other times besides lovemaking?" asks the doctor.

"Oh, sure," says the guy. "It can happen anytime. I can pick up a date and be driving in my car with her when, suddenly, without any warning, this huge, loud fart will erupt and the woman will be totally shocked and I'll be completely embarrassed. As I said, though, at *least* they don't smell. But it can happen anytime anywhere—in a restaurant during a romantic dinner, in a movie theater right at the quietest moment of the film . . . they just blast out. They're so *loud*, Doc, you gotta help me!"

"Now, calm down," says the doctor, "let's take this one step at a time. First of all, I want to examine you. Turn around, drop your drawers, and bend over."

The guy does this, and as the doctor leans in to begin the examination on the man's exposed butt, all of a sudden there is this loud gigantic BOOM! that rattles the walls of the office.

"Okay," says the doctor, leaning back and straightening his hair. "I can see right away that you're going to need an operation."

The guy looks around and says, "Oh no, you mean I'm going to need an operation on my rear end?"

"No," says the doctor, "on your nose."

Q: What's the difference between an oral thermometer and a rectal thermometer?
A: The taste.

A Polish guy decides that he wants to try ice fishing. He gets a fishing rod, a stool, a bucket of bait, and a saw. He goes out onto the ice, puts the bucket down, sits on the stool, gets out his saw, and is about to start cutting, when a deep, loud voice comes booming out from overhead: "DO NOT CUT A HOLE IN THE ICE!"

The Polish guy is startled and quickly looks straight up. Then he looks all around him, but he doesn't see where the voice is coming from. He then replaces the saw on the ice and is about to begin his first cut, when the loud voice once again booms out, "DO NOT CUT A HOLE IN THE ICE!"

The Polish guy jumps up, looks all around, then up in the air again, but he still can't figure out where the voice is coming from. So he settles back in, and is about to start cutting for the third time, when the voice commands, even louder this time, "I REPEAT! DO NOT CUT A HOLE IN THE ICE!"

Now the Polish guy is certain that the voice is coming from directly overhead. He looks up and says, "Who *are* you?"

The voice answers loudly, "THIS IS THE RINK MANAGER! DO NOT CUT A HOLE IN THE ICE!"

■▀■

As unlikely as it may seem, a woman actually told this to me. She said, "Did you know that PMS is mentioned in the Bible?"

I was really surprised. "It is?" I asked incredulously.

"Yeah," she replied. "In the Bible it says, 'Mary rode Joseph's ass all the way to Bethlehem.'"

A cabdriver and a priest die at the same time and they meet at the gates of Heaven. Saint Peter looks at the cabdriver and says, "Just go right in." Saint Peter then turns to the priest. "You're going to have to wait a few hours," he tells him, "but then you, too, will be admitted into Heaven."

"Wait a second," says the priest. "What's going on here? You're letting *him* in before *me*? I'm a *man of God* and he's just a *cabdriver*! And a *New York one at that!*"

So Saint Peter says, "Father, you have to understand that up here we go by results. Now, you have to admit that on Sunday mornings when you were giving your sermons, two-thirds of your congregation was asleep."

The priest rather sheepishly replies, "Well, yes, I guess that is true."

"Now, with this cabdriver here," says Saint Peter, "not only did he *never* have anyone *sleeping* in the back of his cab, but he actually had many people *praying*!"

Q: What do you call a woman without an asshole?
A: Single.

Q: What do a linoleum tile and a woman have in common?
A: If you lay it right, you can walk all over it forever.

Two men are hiking through the woods when they notice that a huge grizzly bear has begun to follow them. They can see by the way the animal is licking his chops that he is hungry. The bear keeps looking at them, and it soon becomes very obvious how he wants to satisfy his hunger.

The bear starts moving more quickly, and the two men begin walking faster and faster, trying to be as nonchalant as they can. Finally, one of the men can't take it any longer. He sits down on the ground and quickly takes his sneakers out of his backpack. He then begins to rapidly change from his hiking boots into his running shoes.

"Are you crazy?" exclaims the other man. "You can't outrun a grizzly!"

"I know," says the man as he finishes tying his sneakers, "but all I have to do is outrun *you*!"

Q: What do you get when you play a country song backward?

A: You get your wife back, you get your job back, you stop drinking . . .

A young Jewish man falls in love with a Native American woman and they decide to get married. When his mother hears the news, however, she is extremely distressed because she wanted him, of course, to marry a nice Jewish girl.

When she hears that not only is he marrying this Native American girl but has decided to live with her on the reservation, the mother becomes so upset that she refuses to even speak to the boy, practically disowning him.

After a year, the son telephones the mother to tell her that he and his wife are expecting a child. The mother is happy for him, but there is still quite a bit of tension in the air.

Nine months later, the son calls the mother again. "Mom," he says, "I just wanted you to know that last night my wife gave birth to a healthy baby boy. I also wanted to tell you that we've talked it over and have decided to give the boy a Jewish name."

Upon hearing this, the mother is overjoyed. "Oh, son, this is wonderful," she gushes. "I've been waiting for this moment all my life. You have made me the happiest woman in the world."

"That's great, Mom," replies the son.

"And what," asks the mother, "is the baby's name?"

The son proudly replies, "Smoked Whitefish!"

Since my first New York Cabdriver's Joke Book *was published, an entirely new genre of jokes has arrived upon the scene: blonde jokes. Now, not only do blondes have more* fun, *they're* funnier, *too!*

Q: What do blondes and beer bottles have in common?
A: They're both empty from the neck up.

Q: What do a peroxide blonde and a Boeing 747 have in common?
A: They both have black boxes.

Q: What do blondes and turtles have in common?
A: Once they're on their backs, they're screwed.

■ ▪ ▪

*I had a guy in my cab who told me that he had a
friend who was a comedian. "My friend," said the guy,
"was going up to Harlem to perform in a club at mid-
night last Saturday night. He asked me to go with him,
but I said, 'Are you crazy? You're a white guy, and
you're going up to Harlem that late at night?' But he
said, 'Aw, everything will be all right.' So he went up
there, and you know what happened?"*

"He got robbed?" I asked.

*The guy, in a very serious tone, said, "Somebody stole
his act."*

*This same guy then said to me, "You know, I'm a
comedy writer, too. As a matter of fact, I'm working on
a joke for David Letterman. It's a great joke. I have it
almost finished except for one line."*

▪ ▪ ▪

Back when Dan Quayle was vice president he
was asked by a reporter who his two favorite black
leaders were. "Well," he answered, "my *first*
favorite was Martin Luther King because he was the
leader of the entire civil rights movement. My *second* favorite black leader was that guy, Malcolm the
tenth."

▪ ▪ ▪

A woman is out on the golf course for her very first time, and she's having great difficulty. Every shot either slices or hooks, and she can't seem to get any shots that come close to landing on the fairway. A golf pro happens to walk by and sees her struggling. As she gets more and more frustrated, he walks up to her and says, "Excuse me, ma'am, but I think I can help you with that."

"You can?" says the woman, tears beginning to well up in her eyes.

"Sure I can. Don't you worry about a thing," comforts the golf pro. "Here, I'll show you." With that, he reaches his arms around her and grabs the club, his hands on top of hers. "You hold the club like this," he instructs. "Now, it might make it a little easier for you, if you think of holding it like you hold your boyfriend's . . . uh . . . male member."

"Ooooh," replies the woman, the lightbulb going off in her head. She looks the golf pro straight in the eye, smiles, grips the club, and WHACK! She hits the ball three hundred and fifty yards down the fairway.

"Wow!" shouts the golf pro, "that was fantastic! Arnold Palmer can't even hit it like that! That was incredible! Now try it again," he says, "but *this* time, take the club out of your *mouth*."

Q: How many men does it take to screw in a lightbulb?
A: Three. One to screw in the bulb, and two to listen to him brag about the screwing part.

Two women are walking through the forest when they suddenly hear a voice say, "Ladies! Ladies!" They look all around them, but they don't see anyone. Then they hear it again. "Ladies! Ladies! Down here!" They look down and see a small pond with a frog sitting on a lily pad.

One of the ladies asks the frog, "Was that *you*?"

"Yes" is the frog's reply.

The two women are in shock. "How can you talk to us?" they ask. "You're a *frog*."

"I got turned into a frog by a wicked witch," explains the frog. "I'm really a fantastic jazz saxophone player."

"Really?" exclaims one of the women. "Is that true?"

"Yes," answers the frog, "and all it will take is one kiss from either of you, and I will immediately change back into a fantastic jazz saxophone player."

Right away, one of the women gets down on her knees, reaches out across the pond to the lily pad, and gently picks up the frog. Then she stands, quickly puts the frog in her pocket, and starts to walk away.

Her startled friend says, "Hey, wait a minute! Where are you going? He said that if you *kiss* him, he'll turn into a fantastic jazz saxophone player!"

"Are you crazy?" replies the other woman. "I can make a *lot* more money with a talking frog than I can with a fantastic jazz saxophone player!"

Q: Why do WASPs love to fly on commercial airlines?
A: For the food.

Q: What did the little WASP boy shout when he saw his school burning down?
A: "MY HOMEWORK!"

A guy goes into his regular pub and sits down at the bar. He says to the bartender, "Give me a martini."

The bartender says to him, "A martini? That's not your drink. You always drink tequila."

"No, no, no," says the guy, "not anymore. You see, every time I drink tequila I blow Chunks."

The bartender looks at the guy sympathetically and says, "That's not such a big deal. That happens to a *lot* of people when they drink tequila."

"You don't understand," says the guy. "Chunks is my dog."

Q: What do you call a brunette walking down the street between two blondes?
A: Interpreter.

Donald Trump is standing in an elevator on his way up to the penthouse (of course), and the only other person in there with him is a woman in a tight red dress. The woman moves over close to him and says, "You are so amazing, Mr. Trump. You're so fantastically rich and so unbelievably sexy that I would just love to go down on you, right here and right now!"

Donald Trump looks over at her and says, "What's in it for me?"

Q: What do you get when you cross LSD with a birth control pill?

A: A trip without the kids.

✦✦✦

Two WASPy society ladies are trying to outsnob each other while having tea. "In Boston," says the first one, "we place our emphasis *entirely* on breeding."

"In Philadelphia," replies the other one, "we think it's a lot of fun, but we do other things too."

✦✦✦

A woman dies, and when she gets to heaven she says to Saint Peter, "Would it be possible for me to get together with my dear departed husband? He died many years ago."

Saint Peter asks, "What was his name?"

The woman replies, "John Smith."

"Gee," says Saint Peter, "we've got a lot of John Smiths up here. But sometimes we can identify people by their last words. Do you happen to remember what his last words were?"

The woman thinks for a moment, then says, "Oh yes! I remember them! He said that if I ever slept with another man after he was gone, he would roll over in his grave."

"Oh!" says Saint Peter. "You mean *Whirling* John Smith!"

A drunk is driving through the city and his car is weaving violently all over the road. An Irish cop pulls him over. "So," says the cop to the driver, "where have you been?"

"I've been to the pub," slurs the drunk.

"Well," says the cop, "it looks like you've had quite a few."

"I did all right," the drunk says with a smile.

"Did you know," says the cop, standing up straight and folding his arms, "that a few intersections back, your *wife* fell out of your car?"

"Oh, thank heavens," sighs the drunk. "For a minute there, I thought I'd gone deaf!"

Q: What's the difference between a coffin and a cello?

A: A coffin has the dead guy on the inside.

Two neighbors are standing in their front yards talking over the fence. One of the neighbors is a Polish guy, and the other man says to him, "You know, pal, you really ought to do something about getting some curtains. I mean, I sit in my living room watching television, I look through my window, and I see you and your wife making love practically every night."

The Polish guy angrily says, "You're full of shit!"

"Oh, yeah?" says the neighbor. "Well, just last night I was in my living room and I could see right into your window, and there was your wife giving you a blow job!"

"Now I *know* you're lying!" says the Polish man. "I wasn't even *home* last night!"

Q: What's the difference between a trampoline and an accordion?
A: You have to take off your shoes before you jump on a trampoline.

A writer, director, and network executive are in the kitchen together making stew. When they finish it, the writer gets a spoon and takes a taste. "Mmm," he says, "it's pretty good. I'm just going to add a little salt." So he picks up the saltshaker and sprinkles some salt into the stew.

Then the director takes a spoonful. "Yeah," says the director, "it's not too bad. Let me just put a little pepper in there." He grabs the pepper and sprinkles some in.

Then the network executive pulls a chair over next to the stove, gets up on the chair, and starts pissing into the stew.

"Hey!" cry the writer and director simultaneously. "What the hell are you doing?"

The network executive looks down at them and replies, "I'm just trying to improve it."

A man calls his wife from the emergency room. He tells her that his finger got cut off at the construction site where he was working.

"Oh, my goodness!" cries the wife. "The whole finger?"

"No," replies the man, "the one next to it."

One day a lawyer receives a telephone call at his office. "Hello," he hears a woman say. "Do you know who I am?"

Not recognizing her voice, he says, "Um . . . refresh my memory."

"We met at a party a couple of months ago. We talked for a while and you said I was really cool. Then we danced together and it was really sensual.

You said again that I was really cool. Then we went back to your place and we made love all night long."

"Oh yes," says the lawyer, "I remember now. How are you?"

The woman replies, "Well, I discovered that I got pregnant that night, and I've decided that I'm going to kill myself."

"Say," exclaims the lawyer, "you really *are* cool!"

Q: What's the smartest thing to ever come out of a woman's mouth?
A: Einstein's dick.

Q: What is the difference between a penis and a prick?
A: A penis is the male sex organ, and a prick is someone who owns one.

A deaf couple on their wedding night are nuzzling together. The shy bride taps her husband on the shoulder and signs to him, "How should I let you know when I want to make love?"

The husband signs back, "Just pull on my penis once."

So the woman giggles, and nuzzles up against her husband again. A few moments later, she taps him again. When he looks over at her, she signs, "How should I let you know when I *don't* want to make love?"

The man signs to her, "Just pull on my penis forty or fifty times."

■■■

Q: How many Microsoft employees does it take to change a lightbulb?
A: None. We'll just declare darkness the new standard.

■■■

Frequently, people will ask me if I have heard the latest weather forecast, and I always have to tell them the same thing: "I never pay attention to what the weathermen say. I find that they are wrong so often that you would be just as well off if you flipped a coin."

It is still amazing to me that with all their sophisticated equipment they are unable to predict the weather any more accurately than they do. One night I was talking to a woman, and we were in total agreement about this whole issue.

I said to her, "I don't know of any other job where you can be wrong so often and get paid so much."

"You're right," she agreed. "As a matter of fact, the only difference between us and the weathermen is that we have windows!"

■■■

In the late 1940s, a couple from New York travels to Budapest for their honeymoon. On their last night there, they are walking around the streets and quaint back alleys of the Old World city, when they come upon a small theater. On the marquee it reads:

Appearing Tonight! The Great Shlomo!

The young couple go in and they find themselves in a tiny little theater with folding chairs and about three people in the audience. There is a small spotlight illuminating the stage, and as the newlyweds take their seats a pretty female assistant in a skimpy costume comes out and places three walnuts on a table. She then walks unceremoniously offstage. The couple hears an announcer's voice coming over a small, tinny loudspeaker, "Ladies and gentlemen, The Great Shlomo!"

The small red curtains part, and out comes a short, little man who resembles Dracula, with the slicked-back jet-black hair and a big long cape. The Great Shlomo, with a flamboyant fanfare, whips open his cape and reveals a huge penis with a massive hard-on the size of a large sausage. He walks up to the table, and with his hard-on he quickly cracks open the three walnuts BOOM! BOOM! BOOM! and the music hits a resounding TA-DAAAAH! There is a smattering of applause and the show is over.

Fifty years later, the couple decides that they want to relive their honeymoon, so they go back to Budapest. It is their first time in the city in fifty years, and at the end of their week there, they are walking through the streets, discussing how much the city has changed. They see a narrow street that looks familiar, so they turn down the little lane. What should they see but the same small theater from so many years ago. The marquee reads:

The Great Shlomo!

They turn to each other. "Could it be?"

"Maybe it's his son!"

"We have to go see."

They walk into the tiny old theater and it looks the same, except that it looks fifty years older. Some of the folding chairs are broken, the spotlight is rather dim, and they are the only two people in the audience. As they sit down, they see the rather dumpy-looking female assistant in her skimpy let-out costume slowly hobble over to the center of the stage. She takes out three coconuts, places them on the table, and walks slowly offstage. As soon as she is in the wings, a raspy voice comes through the crackling speaker: "Ladies and gentlemen, The Great Shlomo!"

The tattered, faded, red curtains part, and out comes The Great Shlomo. His hair is now white, and he also is moving very slowly. Once he gets to the table, though, he suddenly whips open his cape and there is the same massive hard-on. BOOM! BOOM! BOOM! He cracks open the three coconuts in rapid succession.

The couple can't believe it. They decide that they must talk to this man. They go backstage and meet The Great Shlomo in his dressing room. The wife says, "Shlomo! We saw you fifty years ago on our honeymoon. We can't believe that you're still at it!" Shlomo smiles and nods appreciatively.

"There's one thing that puzzles us, though," the husband says. "Fifty years ago you were cracking open walnuts. Now you are cracking open coconuts. How come?"

"Well," says The Great Shlomo in a soft voice, "many years have passed, and to be quite honest, my eyesight isn't what it used to be."

■▼■

Q: Why do bagpipers walk when they play?
A: They're trying to get away from the noise.

■▼■

A man is sitting at the bar in his local tavern, furiously imbibing shots of whiskey. One of his friends happens to come into the bar and sees him. "Lou," says the shocked friend, "what are you doing? I've known you for over fifteen years, and I've never seen you take a drink before. What's going on?"

Without even taking his eyes off his newly filled shot glass, the man replies, "My wife just ran off with my best friend." He then throws back another shot of whiskey in one gulp.

"But," says the other man, "I'm your best friend!"

The man turns to his friend, looks at him through bloodshot eyes, smiles, and then slurs, "Not anymore!"

Q: What's the difference between worry and panic?
A: About twenty-eight days.

An old rabbi is talking with one of his friends and says with a warm smile, "I gladdened seven hearts today."

"Seven hearts?" asks the friend. "How did you do that?"

The rabbi strokes his beard and replies, "I performed three marriages."

The friend looks at him quizzically. "Seven?" he asks. "I could understand six, but . . ."

"What do you think" says the rabbi, "that I do this for *free*?"

Q: What's the definition of 'vagina'?
A: The box a penis comes in.

A young man walks into a drugstore and goes up to the counter. "I'd like a dozen condoms," he proudly announces to the pharmacist. "I've been going out with this really hot babe. We've fooled around a lot, but we haven't actually gone all the way yet. But I think that tonight is going to be the night. I've got her really hot for me now." With that, the young man pays the druggist and swaggers out of the store.

That night the young man arrives at his girlfriend's house to take her out. She meets him outside on the front porch and says, "Since you've never met my parents, they invited you to come in and have dinner with us. After dinner we can tell them that we're going to the movies or something, so that we can get off to spend some time alone." She gives him a wink and leads him into the house.

The family is already seated at the dinner table, and after the introductions are made, they sit down. The young man says to the family, "Would you mind if I say grace tonight?"

The mother says, "Why, I think that would be a lovely idea."

They all bow their heads, and the young man prays,

"Dear Lord, we ask that you bless this food, and that you may always keep us aware of the spirit of forgiveness that was so important in the teachings of Christ. Let us always remember His words, 'To err is human, but to forgive is divine.' In Jesus' name we pray, Amen."

"That was very nice," says the mother, and the family begins to eat. The girl leans over to the young man and whispers, "You didn't tell me that you're so religious."

The young man whispers back to her, "You didn't tell me that your father is a pharmacist."

■ ■ ■

Q: What do you call children born in a whorehouse?
A: Brothel sprouts.

■ ■ ■

An inveterate gambler is always spending money on gambling. Every dime that he gets he blows in Vegas or at the racetrack. One day his wife gets very ill, and she gets rushed to the hospital. The man goes to his friend. "You've gotta help me," he pleads, "I need some money to pay for these hospital bills."

His friend refuses. "I'm not going to give you money. You'll just blow it betting on the horses."

"No, I won't! I promise!" says the gambler. "I've *got* money for the horses."

■ ■ ■

Q: What do you get when you cross an impressionist painter and a New York City cabdriver?

A: You get Vincent Van Go Fuck Yourself!

Two horses are talking, and one of them says to the other, "You know, during the third race today, just as I was going around the curve at the far end of the track, I slipped on this muddy spot and fell down. I scraped my stomach and fell right on my balls. It really hurt!"

"You know, I don't believe it," says the other horse. "Today during the *fifth* race, I was going around that same curve and I slipped at that same spot, scraped my knees, and fell right on my balls. It was really painful! What a coincidence!"

A dog who happens to be walking by turns to the horses and says "I'm really sorry to interrupt, but I couldn't help overhearing what the two of you were saying. This is very strange. You see, I was in the dog race today, and just as I was going around the bend I slipped on a wet spot, scraped my nose, and then fell right on *my* balls. It was excruciating! Once again, I'm so sorry to interrupt, but I just can't believe the coincidence!"

The dog walks off, and one of the horses turns to the other one and says, "What do you know about that! A *talking dog*!"

■■■

Q: Why did the punk rocker cross the road?
A: He was stapled to a chicken.

■■■

Fidel Castro is giving a speech in front of a crowd of one hundred thousand people. "Since I've been in power," he says dramatically, "we have built two hundred new schools—"

He is suddenly interrupted by a man walking through the crowd loudly shouting out, "Peanuts! Popcorn!"

With some effort, Castro regains his composure. "As I was saying, since I've been in power, we have built over three hundred new hospitals—"

"Peanuts! Popcorn!" the man cries out, continuing to pass through the crowd.

Once again, Castro recovers and latches back onto his train of thought, but his temper is beginning to rise. "Since I've been in power, we have built over five hundred—"

"Peanuts! Popcorn!" the man shrieks.

Castro can take it no more, and he screams angrily into the microphone, "If that capitalistic bastard yells 'Peanuts! Popcorn!' one more time, I'm going to kick his ass all the way to Miami!"

With an enormous roar that almost knocks Castro off his feet, a hundred thousand people scream, "Peanuts! Popcorn!"

■▼■

Q: Did you hear what happened to the Polish ice hockey team?
A: They drowned during spring training.

■▼■

A tour group is being guided through a factory that manufactures all types of rubber products, everything from tires to rubber bands. The highlight of the tour is watching the latex condoms being peeled off the penis-shaped molds, rolled up, and slipped into foil packets.

The guests are surprised, however, to notice that every so often, before the condoms are packaged, a man with a pin takes a random rubber off the assembly line and pokes a tiny hole in it.

One of the visitors cries out in shock to the tour guide, "Hey, why is he doing that? Don't they know that those pinholes will cause thousands of unwanted pregnancies?"

"Yeah," says the tour guide, "but just think of what it does for our *nipple* division!"

Q: What's the difference between an Italian-American Princess and a Jewish-American Princess?
A: With an Italian-American Princess, the jewels are fake and the orgasms are real.

There is a big convention in Switzerland for doctors from all over the world. At the end of the first day, after listening to all the introductory lectures, some of the doctors go out together for a drink.

As they begin talking, a little national rivalry begins to surface. A Swedish doctor proclaims, "In Sweden, our medicine is so advanced that we can take a kidney out of one person, put it in another, and have him out looking for work in six weeks."

"Big deal," says a Russian doctor. "In the USSR we can take a lung out of one person, put it in someone else, and have him looking for work in four weeks."

"I hate to show you up," says a German doctor,

"but in my clinic in Berlin, we can take half of a heart out of one man, put it into another man, and have both of them looking for work within two weeks."

"Are these the latest medical developments in your countries?" asks the American doctor. "That's all? Why, in our country, a number of years ago we took an asshole out of Hollywood, put him in the White House, and in only one day the whole country was out looking for work."

A very wealthy man says to his wife, "Honey, if I lost all my money, would you still love me?"

"Of course I would," replies the wife. "But I'd *miss* you . . ."

A barber is standing in his shop late one afternoon when a Polish man walks in. The Pole is wearing a pair of headphones, and when he sits down in the barber's chair, the barber asks him, "Could you please take the headphones off now?"

The Polish man gets a look of panic on his face. "Oh no!" he says. "I can't take the headphones off. If I do, I'll die!"

"Come on, now," replies the barber, "you can't expect me to give you a haircut while you're wearing headphones."

"Just cut around them," the Polish man says.

"That's ridiculous!" says the barber. "I'm not going to do that."

"All right," replies the Polish man as he starts to get up out of the chair. "I'll just go somewhere else."

"No, no, sit back down," says the barber, thinking of how slow his day has been. "I'll cut your hair." He proceeds to give the man a haircut, but it is very difficult cutting around the earphones, and it takes him twice as long as a regular haircut. When he is done, the Polish man pays him and leaves.

The next day, another Polish man comes into the barbershop, and he is also wearing a set of headphones. The barber says to him, "Are you going to take those headphones off so I can give you a normal haircut?"

"No, I can't!" exclaims the Polish man with a look of terror. "If I take them off, I'll die! You have to cut around them."

The barber grumbles, but since it has been another slow day, he agrees to do it. Once again, it takes him a long time to cut the man's hair, and the barber is very frustrated with the difficulty of having to maneuver around the earphones.

The following day, another Polish man walks into the barbershop, and he is also wearing headphones. "Don't tell me," the barber says to him. "You can't take the headphones off or you'll die, so I have to cut around them. Right?"

The Polish man looks relieved. "Yeah," he replies, "that's right!" He sits down in the chair and is expecting his haircut, but the barber is feeling extremely annoyed.

The barber walks around behind the man, and thinks to himself, "This is ridiculous. I'm gonna show this guy that he's *not* going to die if I take his headphones off." The barber reaches slowly up to the man's head, then suddenly yanks the headphones off.

The Polish man immediately clutches his throat with both hands and starts making gasping and choking sounds. He starts to turn blue, then falls out of the barber chair onto the floor. Within moments, the Polish man is dead. The barber is totally shocked. "Oh my God!" he cries out. "What have I done?"

The barber suddenly realizes that he is still holding the headphones in his hands. He puts them up to his ears and hears a voice saying, "Breathe in, breathe out . . . Breathe in, breathe out . . ."

A man goes to the doctor and tells him, "Doc, I'm having a really hard time controlling my bladder."

The doctor says, "Get off my new carpet! Now!"

A seven-year-old boy is sitting at the dinner table with his parents. Suddenly he announces, "Me and Janie are going to get married!"

"Oh?" says the mother. "And how old is Janie?"

"Five," replies the boy.

"Well," says the father, "what are you going to do for money?"

"I get fifteen cents a week allowance," says the

son, "and Janie gets ten cents. We figured that if we put them together, we'd be okay."

"I see," says the father. "But what are you going to do if you have children?"

"Well," says the boy, "so far we've been lucky."

Q: Why do you bury lawyers a thousand feet under the ground?

A: Because deep down, they're probably all right.

Two law partners hire a new cute young secretary, and a contest arises between them as to who can bed her first, even though they're both already married. Eventually one of them scores with her, and his partner is quite eager to hear how things went. "So what did you think?" asks the partner.

"Aah," replies the first lawyer, "my wife is better."

Some time goes by, and then the second lawyer goes to bed with the secretary. "So," asks the first guy, "what did *you* think?"

The second guy replies, "You're right."

Two lawyers are standing at a bar having a drink together. Suddenly, a beautiful woman walks into the room. One of the lawyers leans over to the other one and whispers, "Man, I sure would love to screw *her*."

The other lawyer whispers back, "Out of what?"

◆◆◆

Q: What's the definition of a crying shame?
A: A busload of lawyers going off a cliff with three empty seats.

◆◆◆

A lawyer goes to the doctor because he is not feeling well. After examining him, the physician says to the lawyer, "Before I tell you anything, I would like for you to be examined by my colleague in the next office, just to get a second opinion." The lawyer is introduced to the other doctor, then goes through another complete physical examination. When it is over, the physician tells him to sit in the waiting room until the first doctor calls him back into his office.

A few minutes later he is brought in, and as the lawyer takes a seat across from the doctor's desk, he begins to feel a bit nervous. Both doctors are sitting there behind the desk, with very serious looks on their faces. The first doctor says to the lawyer, "My colleague and I have examined you and we have come to the same conclusion: You have a very rare and incurable disease. You will die in two weeks, and it will be a very slow and painful death."

The other doctor suddenly turns toward the first

doctor, looking very surprised. "Why did you tell him that?"

"Well," replies the first doctor, "I felt that he had the right to know."

"Yeah," whines the other doctor, "but *I* wanted to be the one to tell him."

■▪▪"

Q: How can you get a blonde to marry you?
A: Tell her she's pregnant.

■▪▪"

Two old Jewish men are strolling down the street one day when they happen to walk by a Catholic church. They look over and see a big sign posted on the front of the church that says, "Convert to Catholicism—Get $10."

One of the Jewish men stops walking and stares at the sign. His friend turns to him and says, "Murray, what's going on?"

"Abe," replies Murray, "I'm thinking of doing it."

Abe says, "What are you, crazy?"

Murray thinks for a moment and says, "Abe, I'm gonna do it." With that, Murray strides purposefully into the church.

Abe waits on the sidewalk, and in about twenty minutes Murray comes walking out with his head bowed. "So," asks Abe, "did you get your ten dollars?"

Murray looks up at him and says, "Is that all you people think about?"

Q: What do they call 69 in China?
A: Two Can Chew.

Lord Nelson, the famous British naval commander, is standing on the bridge of his ship talking with his ensign. All of a sudden, from atop the mainsail, the lookout yells down, "Four French frigates off the port stern, sir!"

Admiral Nelson turns to his ensign and says, "Fetch my red jacket."

His ensign replies, "But, sir, if you wear red the enemy is sure to see you! It will be much easier for them to fire upon you from their ships!"

"Yes, yes," says the Admiral, "but should I be hit and should I bleed, the red will absorb the blood and my men will think nothing is wrong, and continue fighting."

The ensign says, "Of *course*! Very good, sir!" He

snaps to attention, salutes smartly, and runs off to get the jacket.

He brings back the red jacket, and Lord Nelson puts it on. About fifteen minutes pass, and the lookout atop the mainsail cries down, "*Forty* French frigates off the port stern, sir!"

Admiral Nelson turns to his ensign and says, "Fetch me my brown trousers."

Q: How does a woman in New York get rid of cockroaches?
A: She asks them for a commitment.

A Texan is in New York on business, and at the end of his first day he decides to relax a little. He goes into a bar wearing his ten-gallon hat and right away this beautiful woman says to him, "Wow, that's a pretty big hat that you've got on."

"Well, ma'am," replies the Texan, tipping his hat, "I'm from Texas, and they make *everything* big down in Texas."

They begin to talk, and after a while the woman invites the man to come back to her apartment with her. When they get there, the woman says to the man, "Why don't you get more comfortable and take off your boots?" The Texan pulls them off, and when he puts them down on the floor, the woman says, "Wow, those are big boots!"

"Like I told you," says the man, "I'm from Texas and they make *everything* big in Texas."

Then the woman suggests to the man, "Well, why don't you *really* get comfortable and take off all your clothes?"

The Texan is only too happy to oblige. When he takes off his pants, the woman looks down between his legs and is amazed. "Oh, my goodness!" she exclaims. "That's some equipment you've got there!"

"Like I said, ma'am," he replies, "*everything's* big in Texas."

One thing leads to another, and pretty soon they decide to go all the way. As they start actually having sex, the Texan says to the woman, "So what part of Texas did you say you were from?"

Q: What should you do when a pit bull starts humping your leg?

A: Fake an orgasm.

Three guys—a Frenchman, a Jew, and a Polish man—die and go to heaven. They meet Saint Peter at the gate, and he says to them, "Before I can let you in I'm going to give you a phrase, then you have to tell me the word that completes that phrase, and then you have to spell the word correctly. Saint Peter turns to the Frenchman and says, "Old MacDonald had a . . ."

The Frenchman says, "Villa! V-I-L-L-A."

"Nah," says Saint Peter, "that's not it." He turns to the Jewish man and says, "Old MacDonald had a . . ."

The Jew replies, "Condo! C-O-N-D-O."

Saint Peter says, "Nope! Sorry."

The Polish guy says, "Old MacDonald had a . . . FARM!"

Saint Peter exclaims, "That's right! Spell it!"

The Pole says, "E-I-E-I-O!"

Confucius say, "Man with hole in pocket feel cocky all day."

One afternoon, two friends happen to meet as they are walking down Broadway. One of them says, "Hey, Tom! How're ya doin'?"

Tom says, "Oh, hi, Murray. Gee, I'm not really doing so well."

Murray replies, "What's the matter?"

"I just went to the dentist," explains Tom, "and he told me that I'm going to have to get my teeth capped. It's gonna cost me *five thousand dollars*!"

"Five thousand dollars!" exclaims Murray. "That's a lot of money! You should go see Dr. Feinman. As a matter of fact, his office is right up here on Broadway, just a couple of blocks north. He only charges five *hundred* dollars for a teeth-capping job."

Tom says, "Five hundred compared to five thousand? Come on, we both know that you get what you pay for. How can it be so cheap? He must not be very good."

"No, he's great!" replies Murray. "He's—Wait a minute! There's Al Cohen across the street! He had *his* teeth done by Dr. Feinman. HEY, AL! COME HERE FOR A MINUTE!"

Al looks over from across the street, sees Murray, and comes right over. Murray introduces his two friends and then says, "Al, you had your teeth capped by Dr. Feinman, didn't you?"

"Yeah," answers Al, "I did. About a month ago."

Murrays says to Al, "Look, Tom needs to get his teeth capped too. Tell him what kind of job Dr. Feinman did for you."

"Oh, okay," says Al. "Well, you know, all summer long my son and I have been trying to take a fishing trip together. Last Saturday we just decided on the spur of the moment to drive upstate to our favorite lake and rent a cabin and rowboat, and do some fishing before we completely miss the summer. So we drove up there, but by the time we got to the lake, it was late in the afternoon. We decided, though, to go out for a couple of hours anyway.

"After sitting on the lake and fishing for a little while, we noticed some storm clouds brewing off in the distance. We didn't think much of it, but the wind was really strong that day, and before we knew it, the storm was right on top of us. We started to row back to shore, but it was really scary. Lightning was crackling all around us, rain was pouring down, and huge waves were starting to kick up. Our little boat was being buffeted around on the waves, when one of the oars slipped out of the oarlock and went overboard.

"I knew that if we lost an oar in that storm, we'd be goners, so I reached out to try to grab it out of the water, but I lost my footing and slipped. My balls got caught in the oarlock and I was halfway out of the boat, hanging by my balls. It was unbelievably painful!"

Tom, who has been listening patiently to all of this, finally can't take it anymore. "What the hell," he demands, "does this have to do with your *teeth*?"

Al replies, "At that moment, it was the first time in a month that I wasn't aware that my teeth hurt."

▼▼▼

Q: What does a woman say after her third orgasm?
A: You mean you still don't know?

▼▼▼

A little six-year-old boy is standing on a street corner with a pair of drumsticks, playing air drums. He is having a really good time, waving the sticks around like he's playing, and making verbal drum sounds. "Boom boom, DA! Ba boom boom, DA!"

A little girl about the same age happens to walk by. She is wearing a cute little dress, and when she sees the boy she stops walking and starts staring intently at him. So now he really starts getting into it. "Zagadaga! Zagadaga!" he says, quickly fanning the sticks in front of him. "Diggleda! Diggleda! Diggleda! Psshhhh!"

The little girl points her forefinger at the boy, then turns it upward and wiggles it. "Follow me," she says. They walk a little bit, then the girl leads the boy back behind a large billboard sign. She pulls up her dress and points between her legs. "Eat that!" she commands.

The boy's eyes open wide, and he stammers, "I . . . I . . . I'm not a *real* drummer!"

■■■

Q: What's the difference between a computer and a woman?

A: A computer will accept a three-and-a-half-inch floppy.

■■■

A man in my cab was a lawyer employed by Donald Trump. He told me that he was working on a project in which Mr. Trump wanted to develop a large area on the Upper West Side of Manhattan, right next to the Hudson River. There were plans to build a state-of-the-art television complex, and one of the buildings in the development would be the tallest building in the world.

The lawyer told me that the people in his office were talking about this building so often that they began to abbreviate the term "world's tallest building" by calling it the "WTB."

One night the lawyers were all in attendance at a town meeting to discuss this project, and since this was a very controversial issue, about four or five hundred people from the neighborhood had shown up. The lawyers kept referring to the building as the "WTB," forgetting that not everyone in attendance knew what the term meant.

Finally a woman stood up. She was a typical Upper West Sider, the lawyer told me. She had the whole outfit: the business suit and the running shoes. "Throughout this meeting," she said, "I've been hearing 'WTB' this and 'WTB' that. Is this the QPS that we're talking about here? Is that what it is, the QPS?"

The lawyer told me that he turned to his associates and they were all asking each other, "QPS? Do you know what QPS stands for?"

Finally, someone said to the woman, "What do you mean, QPS?"

The woman replied, "Quintessential Phallic Symbol."

▼▼▼

Q: What do coffins and condoms have in common?
A: They both have stiffs in them, but one's coming and one's going.

▼▼▼

A man walking down the street sees a restaurant with a sign over it. The sign reads:

WE PAY <u>YOU</u> $500 IF WE CAN'T FILL YOUR ORDER.

So the man goes into the restaurant and sits down. He calls the waitress over and says, "Miss, I would like to order an *elephant ear sandwich.*"

The waitress replies, "Just a moment, sir," and rushes back to the kitchen. She goes straight up to the manager and informs him, "Well, you had better get ready to pay that five hundred dollars."

"Why?" says the surprised manager. "What's wrong?"

The waitress tells him, "Some guy just walked in and ordered an elephant ear sandwich."

"Oh, no!" cries the manager, clutching his head. "Did we run out of elephant ears?"

"No," says the waitress, "but we ran out of those *big buns* we serve them on."

■▼■

Q: What do you call a guy who hangs around with musicians?
A: A drummer.

■▼■

A rabbit and a snake are traveling across a meadow when they bump right into each other. "Excuse me," says the rabbit, "I hope that you can pardon my clumsiness. It's just that I'm blind, and I didn't see you in front of me."

"That's all right," says the snake, "because I'm blind too. I can't see anything at all."

So they start talking, and the rabbit says to the snake, "You know, because I've been blind since birth, I really don't even know what kind of animal I am. Could you maybe crawl all over me and tell me about myself?"

"Sure," the snake replies, "I'd be glad to."

The snake then crawls over the rabbit, and when he's done the rabbit says, "Well, what am I?"

"You're furry," says the snake, "you've got a little cotton tail, and you've got long ears. You must be a rabbit."

"Wow, that's great," says the rabbit. "Thanks!"

"You're welcome," replies the snake. "As a matter of fact, I don't know what kind of animal I am, either. Could you maybe do the same for me?"

"Sure," says the rabbit, and he begins to crawl all over the snake. When he's done he says to the snake, "Well, you're slimy, you've got a forked tongue, beady eyes, no ears, and no backbone. You must be a record company executive."

Q: Why did God give women nipples?
A: Because he wanted to make suckers out of men.

A caddy goes up to a golfer and says, "Hey, I've got this great golf ball I can sell you. You can't lose it."

The golfer says, "What do you mean, you can't lose it?"

"You can't lose it," says the caddy.

"Well," says the golfer, "what happens if it goes into the lake?"

"It floats," says the caddy. "You can't lose it."

"What if it gets lost in the rough?" asks the golfer.

"It beeps," says the caddy. "You can't lose it."

"Well, what about at night?"

"It glows in the dark," says the caddy. "You can't lose it."

"That's incredible," says the golfer. "Where did you get it?"

The caddy says, "I found it."

•••

A guy goes up to a Jewish man and says, "How come you Jews always answer a question with a question?"

The Jewish man shrugs his shoulders and replies, "Why shouldn't we?"

•••

Some tourists in the Museum of Natural History are marveling at the dinosaur bones. One of them asks the guard, "Can you tell me how old the dinosaur bones are?"

The guard replies, "They are three million, four years, and six months old."

"That's an awfully exact number," says the tourist. "How do you know their age so precisely?"

The guard answers, "Well, the dinosaur bones were three million years old when I started working here, and that was four and a half years ago."

•••

Q: How do you make God laugh?
A: Tell him your plans.

Then there's the story of the bottomless bartender. Everyone called him Shorty, especially the women, but it wasn't because he had a short memory. It was because he had a tattoo on his penis that said, "Shorty."

What the women didn't realize, though, was that when he got excited, the tattoo said, "Shorty's Restaurant and Pizzeria . . . Featuring the finest in Italian-American cuisine . . . Open 24 hours, seven days a week . . . For free delivery, dial 555-4000 . . . In New Jersey, dial 201 . . . For complete menu, see other side."

But what really made it hard for him was that it was written in Braille.

Note: When verbally telling this joke, pause after saying, "Shorty's Restaurant and Pizzeria." As the laugh that you get begins to die down, add the phrase, "Featuring the finest in Italian-American cuisine." When that laugh starts to fade, say, "Open 24 hours, seven days a week." Keep adding the lines that way and the laughs will build and keep coming! (No pun intended.)

Q: Did you hear about the prostitute with a degree in psychology?
A: She'll blow your mind.

A guitar player, a lead singer, and their road manager are in an elevator. They are riding down from the forty-third floor when the elevator starts making a loud screeching sound and then suddenly comes grinding to a halt. They push buttons and alarms, but nothing seems to work. Finally, after standing in the elevator for twenty minutes, one of the guys says, "Man, I really wish we could get out of here!"

A large puff of smoke appears in the center of the elevator, and when it clears, the three guys are amazed to see a genie standing there. "Greetings," he says. "I am the Elevator Genie. I am empowered to grant three wishes, and since there are three of you, I will grant you each one wish." He turns to the guitar player and asks, "What is your wish?"

The guitar player thinks for a moment, then says, "You know, at this very minute, the Rolling Stones are playing out at the Meadowlands Arena. I would give *anything* to be onstage jamming with them right now!"

"Oh, that's easy," replies the genie, and snaps his fingers. *Poof!* A cloud of smoke envelops the guitarist. When the smoke clears, the guitar player is gone. The genie turns to the lead singer. "And what is your wish?" he asks.

The lead singer doesn't even have to think about it. "Two weeks ago," he says eagerly, "we played a concert out in L.A. There was this blonde in the second row, and I just can't seem to get her out of my mind. I don't know her name, though, where she's from, or anything about her."

The genie smiles. "I know her name, where she's from, and right now she is lying on a California beach in a bikini. At the snap of my fingers, you will be immediately transported to that beach, lying right next to her." And with that, he snaps his fingers and *poof!* The lead singer disappears. The genie turns to the road manager. "And what would you like?" he asks.

The road manager commands the genie, "GET THOSE GUYS BACK HERE, *RIGHT NOW!*"

▼▼▼

Q: Why is Cuba such a mess?
A: It has the island in the Caribbean, the government in Russia, the troops in Angola, and the population in Miami.

A cabdriver says to a beautiful woman in his taxi, "If I gave you some money, would you sleep with me?"

The woman angrily replies, "How *dare* you?"

But before she can say any more, the cabbie quickly says, "Wait a minute, lady, wait a minute! Before you get all upset, let me ask you something. If I was as handsome as a movie star, had the body of a champion athlete, was one of the wealthiest men in the world, and I offered you two million dollars to spend one night with me, *then* would you sleep with me?"

The woman sits back and thinks for a minute. "Well," she says, "if you were *all that*, then I guess I have to admit that I would."

"In that case," says the driver, "will you fuck me for twenty-five bucks?"

"What?" says the indignant woman. "Just what kind of woman do you think I am?"

"We've already established that," replies the cabbie. "Now we're just dickering over price."

Q: What is a Japanese girl's favorite holiday?
A: Erection day.

Bernie is having his annual checkup, and at the end of the examination his doctor proclaims him to be in excellent health. "I wonder if your fine physical condition could be hereditary," the doctor says. "How old was your father when he died?"

"What makes you think he's dead?" asks Bernie. "Pop just turned eighty-five, and he's still going strong."

"Remarkable," says the doctor, "and how long did your grandfather live?"

"Believe it or not, Doc," replies Bernie, "he's a hundred and seven, and next week he's getting married to a twenty-year-old girl."

"At his age!" exclaims the doctor. "Why does he want to marry a twenty-year-old?"

"Doc," replies Bernie, "what makes you think that he *wants* to?"

▼▼▼

Q: How can you tell if a blonde has been using your computer?
A: You find White-Out on the monitor.

▼▼▼

One night I overheard a discussion about shopping between two high school girls. One of them said to the other, "It must have been great growing up with a father who is the head of one of the largest department-store chains in the area!"

"Well, it was kind of nice," answered the other girl, "because we got to go into the store and pick out whatever we wanted. The problem was that very often I didn't like the clothes that the store had, and we weren't allowed to wear anything that didn't come from my father's store.

"My mother used to cheat, though," the girl went on. "She used to buy clothes in other stores and then sew labels in them from dad's store. She never got caught, either!"

◆◆◆

A woman is standing before the judge explaining the grounds for her divorce. "The reason I want to divorce my husband," she says, "is because of his blatant hobosexuality."

"Excuse me," replies the judge, "don't you mean to say 'homo-sexuality'?"

"No," replies the woman. "Hobo-sexuality. He's a bum fuck."

◆◆◆

An elderly couple decide to go on a weekend cruise to celebrate their fiftieth wedding anniversary. As they board the ship, the woman realizes that she has forgotten to bring her hearing aid with her. The couple considers going back and not taking the cruise, but they have already paid the money, so they decide to make the best of it.

When they get to their cabin, however, they encounter another problem. There seems to have been some mix-up, and instead of getting the bridal suite, they have been assigned to a room with bunk beds. As disappointed as they are, they decide not to let it spoil their plans.

That night, they have a wonderful dinner in the ship's restaurant and then they go to the main ballroom and dance for hours. Afterward, the husband and wife go for a romantic walk on the moonlit deck. At the end of the evening, when they finally get back down to their cabin, the man, being of chivalrous nature, offers his wife her choice of the top or bottom bunk bed.

"Up or down?" he asks.

The woman looks at him, and her eyes widen. She immediately rips off her clothes and pulls the man down on top of her. They make love all night long, and the next morning the man wakes up with a smile on his face.

The couple has another nice day on the cruise, and then that night, as they are about to go to bed, the man thinks to himself, "Last night was so wonderful. I don't know why asking her which bunk she wanted had such an effect on her, but if it worked once, maybe it will work again." So he says, "Up or down?"

The woman yanks off her clothes, but this time she throws the man on the bed and jumps on top of him. Once again, they do it all through the night.

The next evening, the cruise ship returns to port.

When the couple arrives home, the first thing the wife does is put her hearing aid back in. "This is so much better," she says. "I really wish I hadn't forgotten it for the cruise."

As the couple is about to get ready for bed, the man is still baffled as to why his question made his wife so wild. He thinks, "Maybe she thought I was asking her which position she preferred for making love. Whatever it was, it worked so well on the boat, I might as well give it a try here at home." So he looks at his wife and says, "Up or down?"

The wife gazes at him quizzically. "What?" she says.

"Up," repeats the man, "or down?"

The wife says to the man, "What in the world are you talking about?"

Now the husband is totally confused. "Well," he says, "on the ship, whenever I said 'Up or down,' you made wild passionate love to me."

"Oooh," replies the wife. "I thought that you were saying, '*Fuck* or *drown*.'"

Q: Did you hear about the bulimic bachelor party?
A: The cake comes out of the girl.

Three guys are sitting around arguing over what has been the greatest invention ever achieved by mankind. The first one says, "The greatest invention has got to be the Cadillac car. When you drive down the street in one, it shows everyone that you have not only class, but style, and they take their hats off when you drive by."

The next fellow says, "Oh man, that's not it. The greatest invention of mankind is the color television. You know, the color television has one hundred-and-forty-seven channel capability, it's got true-life color that's just like being there, and you can watch it any-time of the week, day or night."

The third guy says, "I hate to tell you this, but you're both wrong. The greatest thing that mankind has ever invented is, without a doubt, the thermos jug. Why, if you put something hot in it, it keeps it hot. Then if you put something cold in it, it keeps it cold."

"So what?" say the first man.

"Yeah," adds the second, "what's so great about that?"

"Well," says the third guy, getting very excited, "HOW DOES IT KNOW?"

▼▼▼

Q: What's the difference between Quasimodo and a messy room?
A: You can straighten up a messy room.

▼▼▼

Sometimes there's not much work around. In times like these, this is often *especially* true for ventriloquists. One day, two out-of-work ventriloquists are talking on the phone to each other (without moving their lips) and lamenting their condition. One of them, the older one who has been around the block a few times, says to the younger man, "Just between you and me, I've been moonlighting lately as a medium."

The young ventriloquist is quite impressed. "Really?" he says. "I didn't know that you were psychic!"

"Well, to tell you the truth, I'm not," confesses the older man. "But what I did was rent a storefront and bought a small round table, a crystal ball, and a turban. Then, when people come in, I throw my voice and they think that they're talking to their dead relatives."

"What a great idea!" says the young ventriloquist.

"You should try it too," suggests the first man. "You'll see, it works great."

The next day, the young man goes out, rents a little storefront, and buys a table, a crystal ball, and a turban. He opens up for business, and an hour later a middle-aged woman walks in. She sits down at the table across from the ventriloquist and asks him, "Can you put me in touch with my long-lost husband?"

"I sure can!" he answers. "Why, for just a hundred dollars, you can hear your husband speak to you from behind that curtain over there. Now, I must warn you that his voice might sound a little different, but that's because he's talking to you from the spirit world."

"That's wonderful," says the woman eagerly.

"For a *hundred and fifty* dollars," the ventriloquist says, "you could have a two-way conversation with your husband, and talk back and forth with him."

The woman's voice rises in anticipation as she asks, "You mean, *I* could communicate directly with my dear departed Hubert?"

"Not only *that*," says the ventriloquist, getting just as excited as the woman. "For *two hundred* dollars, you could actually carry on a two-way conversation with your husband while *I'm* drinking a *glass of water*!"

■▀■

Q: What do you call a drummer without a girlfriend?
A: Homeless.

■▀■

A Jewish funeral. Rubenstein has just died. There's a small collection of people there. The rabbi gets up and says, "Ladies and gentlemen. Ve're going to bury Mr. Rubenstein. I know he vasn't the most popular man in the neighborhood, but it's very important in the Jewish tradition that you have to say a few kind vords about a man before you can bury him. So I'm not going to talk about Rubenstein, I'm not going to be critical. Personally I didn't even know him. But if vun of you could be nice enough to say a few vords, ve'll get this over yipsy pipsy, and ve'll be done vit it."

There is a long silence. "Excuse me," says the rabbi, "Mr. Stein, I don't vant to bodder you, but you knew diss man, you lived near him for so many years, perhaps you could say a few kind vords."

Mr. Stein stares straight ahead. "I vouldn't say nothing."

"Excuse me," says the rabbi, "I don't vant to bodder you, Mr. Kornblatt, but you vent to school vit Mr. Rubenstein, you vorked in the same business for so many years, you don't have to make a long speech, you don't have to make a eulogy, you don't have to be Shakespeare, but just a few vords, a sentence, two sentences, somzing, so ve can bury him and all go home."

Kornblatt says, "I've got notting to say about dat man, I don't want to talk about him. Vat I've got to say vouldn't help you. It's better I keep my mouth shut."

The rabbi says, "Ladies and gentlemen, I'm going to have to remind you, the Jewish people, it's a Jewish tradition, you can't bury a man, you can't put him in the earth forever unless somebody could say vun vord, a sentence, somzing, vun kind vord so ve can bury him. Ve'll be here forever. I vouldn't bury him, I'm *telling* you."

There is a long silence again. The rabbi says, "Look, Mr. Goldberg, maybe you could do a mitzvah for us all, you could just say vun kind vord. You knew him, you knew the family, just vun kind vord, Mr. Goldberg."

Goldberg looks up at the rabbi. "Everybody vants to go home," he says, "I'll say vun ting. *His brother vas vorse dan him!*"

‥▼‥

Q: How can you save a lawyer from drowning?
A: Take your foot off his head.

‥▼‥

Three women die at the same moment and are standing in front of Saint Peter at the gates of heaven. Saint Peter says to the first woman, "How much money did you earn during your last year on earth?"

The woman answers, "I worked at an investment banking firm on Wall Street and I earned five hundred thousand dollars."

Saint Peter turns to the second woman and asks her the same question. "Well," she replies, "I was an executive at a large cosmetics corporation and I made two hundred thousand dollars."

"And how much did you earn?" Saint Peter asks the last woman.

She replies, "I made eight thousand dollars."

"Oh," says Saint Peter. "Ballet, jazz, or tap?"

Q: Did you hear about the new Chinese restaurant that has really hot, spicy food?
A: It's called Szechuan fire.

A middle-aged Jewish widow is walking through the park, when she sees a middle-aged man sitting on a bench. The man strikes her fancy, so she goes over and sits down next to him. They sit there in silence for fifteen minutes, so the woman decides that she must take the initiative. She turns to the man and sweetly asks, "Do you like pussycats?"

The man's eyes widen and he turns to her, breaking into a broad smile. "How did you know," he asks, "that my name is Katz?"

Q: What's the difference between L.A. and yogurt?
A: Yogurt has an active culture.

■▼■▼

A guy goes over to his friend's house and knocks on the door. When it opens, though, it is the friend's wife who is standing there. "Oh, hi, Phyllis," says the guy, "is Gary home?"

"No, he's not, Bobby," Phyllis replies, "he won't be home from work for another twenty minutes. Would you like to come in and wait?"

Bobby thinks for a moment and then says, "Yeah, okay. Thanks!"

They go in, sit down, and then suddenly Bobby blurts out, "I know I shouldn't say this, Phyllis, but you've got the most beautiful breasts in the world. As a matter of fact, I would give a hundred dollars if I could take a peek at just *one* of them."

Phyllis is quite taken aback, but after she recovers from her shock, she finds that she's feeling a little bit flattered. Then, thinking of the hundred dollars, she decides, "Oh, what the hell," and opens her bathrobe, exposing one marvelously shaped mound.

Bobby immediately pulls out a hundred-dollar bill and slaps it down on the table. "That was fantastic!" he exclaims.

They sit there in silence for a few moments, then Bobby says to her, "You know, Phyllis, that was so amazing that I would give *another* hundred dollars to see them both together. What do you say?"

Phyllis thinks to herself, and after just a moment's hesitation, she pulls open her robe and lets the guy stare at her perfect pair. After the guy gets a nice long look, Phyllis closes up her bathrobe, then Bobby whips out another hundred-dollar bill. He plops it down on the table and says, "Incredible, just incredible!"

Bobby then gets to his feet and says, "Well, I have to get going. Thanks a lot!"

About fifteen minutes later, Gary arrives home. Phyllis says to him, "Oh, by the way, your friend Bobby dropped by."

"Oh yeah?" says Gary, a little surprised. "Well, tell me, did that jerk drop off the two hundred bucks he owes me?"

■▪■

A termite walks into a bar and asks, "Where's the bar tender?"

■▪■

Albert Einstein is walking around in heaven, when Saint Peter sees him and calls him over to his station at the gate. "Albert," says the saint, "I need to quickly run an errand. Would you mind watching the Gate for me for a few minutes?"

Dr. Einstein kindly answers, "It would be my pleasure."

He takes the seat behind the podium, and a few minutes later a man comes walking over a cloud bank and up to the gate. "Welcome to heaven," says Einstein. "What's your IQ?"

"It's two hundred," replies the man.

"That's great!" exclaims Einstein. "Maybe you can help me finish my grand unified field theory!"

The man says, "I'd love to!"

"Well, I'm watching the Gate for Saint Peter," Einstein explains, "so can you wait for me inside for a few minutes?"

"Sure," replies the man. "I look forward to having the opportunity of working with you!"

A few moments later, another man comes walking over the clouds and Einstein greets him. "Welcome to heaven," he says. "What's your IQ?"

The man answers, "It's one ninety-five, Dr. Einstein."

"Fantastic!" says Einstein. "Could you maybe help us work on my grand unified field theory?"

"It would be an honor, Doctor" is the man's respectfully polite answer.

"Wonderful!" says Einstein. "Please wait for me right inside the gate. You'll find another man there, and I'll be joining you both in just a few minutes."

The man goes in, and Einstein sees a third man coming toward him. When the man gets to the podium, Einstein says, "Welcome to Heaven. What's your IQ?"

The third man replies, "Fifty-eight."

Einstein looks at the man, smiles, and says, "So how about those Dallas Cowboys!"

■▪◆▪■

Just after God invented Adam, he said to his newly created man, "I have some good news for you and some bad news. The good news is that I gave you a very large brain and a very large penis."

Adam exclaims, "That sounds great!"

"The bad news," says God, "is that I only gave you enough blood to operate one of them at a time."

Q: What do George Washington, Thomas Jefferson, and Abraham Lincoln have in common?
A: They were the last three white men to have those last names.

A record producer dies and goes to heaven. He is greeted at the Pearly Gates by Saint Peter, who smiles and says to him, "I'm very happy to welcome you to heaven." And with that, the gates swing open wide and the producer walks in. He is astounded to see that heaven is a state-of-the-art recording studio.

The celestial studio is equipped with tube limiters, a fully digital mixing board with automated faders, wood carved walls, and speakers that are small, but clearer than anything the producer has ever heard on earth.

The producer has barely had time to regain his composure from the swoon that seeing all this unbelievably beautiful equipment has put him in, when Saint Peter says to him, "You are one of those rare individuals who has led such a good life on earth that we are now going to give you a choice. You may either stay here in heaven and live out eternity with us, or, if you wish, you may go to the other place."

"Wow!" exclaims the producer. "That's quite an offer! Not that I would be interested in going to the other place, of course, but . . . just out of curiosity, could I maybe take a peek and see what it looks like?"

"Certainly!" Saint Peter replies.

A trapdoor in the clouds near their feet opens up, and the producer looks down. He finds himself peering directly into the bowels of Hell. What he sees is a long banquet table filled with food, including huge platters of steaks and pork chops. Crowded onto the long table alongside the bounteous food are many bottles of beer, wine, liquor, champagne, and, of course, tequila. Around the table there are many people eating, drinking, and laughing hysterically. An incredible live band with many of the greatest musicians who ever lived is playing some funky, kick-ass R&B. Out on the dance floor are many beautiful, scantily clad men and women rocking to the irresistibly throbbing groove. At another table next to the stage is a large group of people smoking joints and doing lines of cocaine.

"Well," Saint Peter says to the producer, "what is your decision?"

"To tell you the truth, Pete," the producer says, "when I was alive, I worked pretty hard for many years. I kind of feel like I've already done the studio thing for a very long time. I'm really more into relaxing now, so I'm going to choose the other place."

"Suit yourself" is all that Saint Peter says before another trapdoor opens right below the producer's feet. The producer drops quickly down through a long, dark chute, and before he knows it he is thrown through a door and deposited onto the floor of hell. He looks around, and all he sees are flames.

The devil is hiding behind the door, and as it slams shut, the devil takes a pitchfork and rams it up the producer's ass. He then lifts the pitchfork up and starts roasting the producer out over the flames.

The producer cries out, "Hey! Where's all the food and drink? Where's the band and beautiful women? Where's all the smoke and blow?"

The devil looks up at the producer, smiles, and then says, "Nice demo, huh?"

■▼■

Q: What do you get when you kiss a bird?
A: Chirpies. It is a canarial disease that's untweetable.

■▼■

At the Port Authority bus terminal a woman got into my cab. When she told me her destination I could hear that she had a very thick southern accent. Since I had just picked her up at the bus terminal I asked her, "Where are you coming in from?"

She said, "Oh, I live in New York now, but my sister was just up visiting me from Houston. This was her first time visitin' New York and, I swear, if I hadn't taken her out to the airport myself, she never would have gotten home again."

"Oh?" I asked. "Did New York give her a hard time?"

"Well, it was just very different for her," said the woman. "You see, she's very much a fundamentalist, religious-type person, and I knew that New York would be somethin' of a shock to her. So I called her up on the phone a few days before she was going to arrive, and I said, 'Mary Sue, I'm gonna warm you up: FUCK YOU, FUCK YOU, FUCK YOU, FUCK YOU, FUCK YOU, FUCK YOU, FUCK YOU, FUCK YOU! Now, you're gonna hear that a lot once you get up here, and after a while, it just don't mean anything."

Q: What's the difference between capitalism and communism?

A: Under capitalism, man exploits man, whereas under communism, it's the other way around.

A Martian comes to earth, and he has a flat tire on his terrestrial vehicle. He doesn't know what to do, so he starts walking around, and eventually he passes a bagel shop. The bagels look kind of like tires, so he goes into the store. "I'd like one of those tires," he says to the man behind the counter.

"That's not a tire," explains the clerk, "that's a bagel."

"What's a bagel?" says the Martian.

"It's a kind of bread."

The Martian looks at the bagel carefully, and then says, "Okay, I'll try one."

The clerk hands a bagel over the counter, and the Martian cautiously takes a bite.

"How do you like it?" asks the clerk.

"It's not bad," replies the chewing Martian, "although I think it would be better with lox and cream cheese."

Q: Did you hear about the new Barbie doll, "Divorced Barbie"?

A: She comes with Ken's things, too.

One morning, a mother goes into her son's room and says to him, "It's time to get up! It's the first day of the new school year!"

The son scrunches down and pulls the covers up over his head. "I'm not going!" he shouts.

"Why, son," says the mother, "why don't you want to go to school?"

The son answers, "Because all the teachers hate me and all the kids hate me."

"Son," the mother says, "it doesn't matter if the teachers hate you. It doesn't matter if the kids hate you. You have to go to school today because everyone is counting on you. You're the principal!"

Q: What part of a man's body should he never move when dancing with a woman?
A: His bowels.

A koala bear goes into a tavern and sits down at the bar. As he's having his beer, a woman comes up and sits down on the stool next to him. "Hello!" she says.

"G'day," replies the koala.

"You're not from around here, are you?" asks the woman.

"No," says the koala. "I'm from Australia."

"Well, you're kind of cute," says the woman, moving in closer to the little bear.

"You're not so bad yourself," replies the koala.

"How would you like to come up to my apartment?" asks the woman.

"Sounds great," says the bear, and off they go.

As soon as they get inside the apartment, the

koala bear rips the woman's clothes off and throws her on the bed. He then proceeds to go down on her. After about a half hour of this, the bear gets up and starts to walk out.

"Where are you going?" asks the woman.

"Back to the bar," answers the koala.

"You don't seem to understand," says the woman. "I'm a prostitute."

"Prostitute?" says the bear. "What's that?"

"Here," says the woman, and tosses a dictionary at the koala. "Look it up."

The bear flips through the pages, then says, "Here it is! I found it!"

"Now pay particular attention," says the hooker, "to the part of the definition where it says, 'performs sexual favors in return for money.'"

"But," says the Australian animal, "I'm a koala bear."

"So what?" asks the woman. "What's a koala bear?"

"Look it up," says the koala, and tosses the dictionary back to the woman.

She pages through the book until she finds it. "Ah! Here it is," she says.

"Now pay particular attention," says the Koala bear, "to the part of the definition where it says, 'eats bushes and leaves.'"

I heard a woman tell this joke to another woman.

Q: What do a computer and a man have in common?
A: You don't *really* know what it means to you until it goes down on you.

■▼■

Q: What do a condom and a wife have in common?
A: They both spend most of their time in your wallet.

■▼■

A middle-aged Jewish widow is sitting on the beach in Florida sunning herself. A middle-aged man walks by, catches her eye, and sits down near her. She looks over toward him and says, "Pardon me, but I've been living here for five years and I don't recognize your face. Are you new around here?"

"Yeah," the man answers, "I just came in."

The woman asks him, "So where are you from?"

The man shifts uncomfortably, and says, "Yeah, well . . . I . . . um . . . um . . ." and his voice trails off.

So the woman asks, "Well, what do you do?"

"Well, actually," says the man, "I don't do anything. You see, I've been in prison for thirty years."

"Oh my," remarks the woman. "What did you go to prison for?"

The man tells her, "I murdered my wife with an ax."

"Oh," says the woman. "So you're single?"

Q: How can you tell if your roommate is gay?
A: His dick tastes like shit.

B.B. King's wife decides that she is going to make his birthday especially memorable this year. The day before the party, she goes out and gets B.B.'s initials tattooed on her buttocks, one letter on each cheek. The next night, after his big birthday dinner with friends in his favorite restaurant, they go home. As soon as B.B. sits down in his favorite chair, his wife walks up to him and announces, "I have a big surprise for you." With that, she turns around, pulls up her dress, drops her drawers, and bends over.

B.B. stares for a moment at the posterior just inches from his face, and then asks, "Who's Bob?"

Q: What's the worst thing about being an atheist?
A: When you're getting a blow job, you've got no one to talk to.

Three guys are arrested and banished to Siberia. One of them is a Jewish guy, another is Italian, and the third guy is Polish. They're all sentenced to twenty years, but they are each allowed to bring one thing along with them. The Jewish guy wants a telephone, the Italian asks to bring a woman along, and the Polish guy requests twenty thousand cartons of cigarettes.

They are granted their wishes, and then they are all sent away.

Twenty years later, when the three guys are let out, some reporters are waiting to talk to them. The first to be interviewed is the Jewish guy. A reporter asks him, "How was it?"

The Jewish guy says, "Well, I had a phone in the prison, so I was able to do some business. I now have a hundred thousand dollars in the bank."

Then they ask the Italian man how he is. He says, "You see, since I had a woman in jail with me, I now have a big family with lots of bambinos!"

So they turn to the Polish guy and say, "So how was it for you?"

The Polish guy says, "Anybody got a *match*?"

Q: What did the Deadhead say when he stopped taking acid and smoking grass?
A: "This music is *shit*!"

A man gave me this, saying that he had gotten it off the Internet:

Are you a guy?
Take this scientific quiz to determine your Guyness Quotient.

You have been seeing a woman for several years. She's attractive and intelligent, and you always enjoy being with her. One leisurely Sunday afternoon the two of you are taking it easy—you're watching a football game; she's reading the papers—when she suddenly, out of the clear blue sky, tells you that she thinks she really loves you but she can no longer bear the uncertainty of not knowing where your relationship is going. She says she's not asking whether you want to get married, only whether you believe that you have some kind of future together. What do you say?

a. That you sincerely believe the two of you do have a future, but you don't want to rush it.

b. That although you also have strong feelings for her, you cannot honestly say that you'll be ready anytime soon to make a lasting commitment, and you don't want to hurt her by holding out false hope.

c. That you cannot believe the Jets called a draw play on third and seventeen.

Q: What's the difference between a violin and a viola?

A: A viola takes longer to burn.

A woman goes on a game show trying to win the top prize of $50,000. She keeps answering question after question, and the prize money keeps building up. Finally she gets to the last question and the host says, "Okay, now. For fifty-thousand dollars, here is your final question: What are the three most important parts of a man's body?"

Suddenly a loud buzzer sounds. "Oh, I'm sorry," says the host, "our time is up for today. We'll have to come back next week and ask you that question again. If you can answer it correctly, though, you will win fifty-thousand dollars!"

So the woman goes home that night, and her husband is really excited. "Wow, honey!" he exclaims as he hugs her. "You did great! That was fantastic! And just wait until next week! We'll win fifty-thousand dollars!"

So the wife says to him, "Well, tell me, honey. What *are* the three most important parts of a man's body?"

The husband answers, "It's the head, the heart, and the penis."

"Oh, okay," she says. "Great!"

So for the next few days, the husband keeps testing her with the question. She's in the shower when he suddenly sticks his head in around the curtain and barks, "What are the three most important parts of a man's body?"

She quickly replies, "HEAD, HEART, AND PENIS!"

"Great!" says the husband.

All week long he keeps testing her, asking her at the strangest moments, and trying to catch her off guard. But she always gets the right answer.

Finally the big night arrives, and she is very excited as she arrives at the television studio. The lights go on, and as soon as they go on the air, the host says to her, "All right! You've had a week to prepare! Now . . . for fifty-thousand dollars . . . what are the three most important parts of a man's body?"

The studio audience falls to a hush. The hot bright lights are shining down, the cameras push in for a close-up, and the woman starts to get flustered.

"Um . . . um . . . um . . . the . . . the . . . uh . . . the HEAD!"

"That's ONE!" says the host.

"Uh . . . uh . . . uh," stammers the woman, "uh . . . the HEART!"

The host shouts out, "That's TWO!"

Now the woman is so nervous that she can hardly think. "Oh, I know it, I know it," she says, "it's right on the tip of my tongue . . . I could spit it out . . . it's been drilled into me all week . . ."

The host says, "Aaah, that's close enough. You win."

■▼■

Q: How do you get a blonde to laugh on Monday?
A: Tell her a joke on Friday.

■▼■

Being a musician, writer, and artist, and all the while supplementing my income by driving a cab, I met many other struggling people in the arts. I finally got to the point where every time I met a woman who told me that she was an actress, I would ask, "Oh, really? Which restaurant?"

Most of them would reply with "Unfortunately, you're right."

I could definitely relate.

■▼■

Q: What's the difference between a Jewish-American Princess and a freezer?

A: You have to plug in a freezer.

■▼■

Three guys sitting on a park bench all decide to start rating the women walking by. The first woman who goes by happens to be a real knockout, and the first guy says, "Ten!"

"Definitely!" agrees the second guy. "Without a doubt. A ten!"

The third guy says, "Two."

The next woman who walks by is another beauty. "Another ten!" says the first guy.

The second guy says, "I have to admit it, you're right again. Ten!"

"Ummm," says the third guy, deep in thought, "I guess that's a three."

The next woman who comes by is really strutting her stuff. The first guy exclaims, "Wow! Three tens in a row! This is our lucky day!"

The second guy says, "Yeah, we have to remember this spot! One ten after another! This is great!"

"Two" is the third guy's immediate evaluation.

The first guy turns to the third guy and bursts out, "What the hell are you doing? These are gorgeous women. They're all *tens*! Why are you only rating them twos and threes?"

"Well, you see," explains the third guy, "you guys must be using a different system than me. *I'm* trying to think of how many *Clydesdales* it would take to drag her off my *face!*"

A woman goes into a toy store and picks a Barbie doll off the shelf. As she's looking at it, the store manager happens to walk by. "Excuse me, sir," the woman asks the manager, "does Barbie come with Ken?"

"No," the manager replies, "Barbie *fakes it* with Ken. She *comes* with G.I. Joe!"

Q: How many psychiatrists does it take to screw in a lightbulb?
A: Just one, but the lightbulb has to want to change.

Or the alternate version:

Q: How many psychiatrists does it take to screw in a lightbulb?
A: What do *you* think?

A little guy gets on a plane and sits next to the window. A few minutes later, a big, heavy, strong, mean-looking, hulking guy plops down in the seat next to him and immediately falls asleep. The little guy starts to feel a little airsick, but he's afraid to wake the big guy up to ask if he can go to the bathroom. He knows that he can't climb over him, and so the little guy is sitting there, looking at the big guy, trying to decide what to do. Suddenly, the plane hits an air pocket and an uncontrollable wave of nausea passes through the little guy. He can't hold it in any longer and pukes all over the big guy's chest.

About five minutes later the big guy wakes up, looks down, and sees the vomit all over him. "So," says the little guy, "are you feeling better now?"

A man comes home and finds his partner in bed with his wife. "Max!" he exclaims. "I *have* to. But *you* . . . ?"

Two friends who are struggling actors in New York City become taxi drivers to help support their artistic ambitions. After a couple of months of driving, one of the actors gets a part in a movie and is flown out to L.A. When the movie is released, it turns out to be a big hit and the actor goes on to become a big international movie star.

His friend, however, continues to drive a cab and keeps hoping for his big break. All the while, he closely follows his friend's career, sees all his films, and vicariously enjoys his success.

Ten years pass, and one day the famous actor is in New York on a promotional tour and he hails a cab. As luck would have it, the driver turns out to be his old friend, and they are both very surprised and happy to see each other.

After spending a few minutes catching up, the cabdriver says to the star, "Lou, tell me something.

We were in acting classes together for many years. We went to the same auditions, and at that time we were fairly equal in our acting ability. Yet you went out to Hollywood and became a great movie star, and I'm still here, struggling in New York, driving a taxi.

"Lou, is there anything that you have learned over the years that you could tell me about the acting profession? Something that would help me become more like you, a successful actor?"

"Yes, there is," replies Lou, "and I can sum it up in one word."

"Really?" the cabbie says with excitement. "Just one word? What is it?"

"Sincerity," replies Lou.

"Sincerity?" the cabbie asks. "That's it?"

"Yep," says the actor, "*sincerity*. Once you can fake *that*, you can do *anything!*"

■▼■

Did you know that name-dropping is the *worst* thing you can do? Bobby De Niro told me that.

■▼■

After a hard day making the rounds in L.A., an actor drives home to his house in the Hollywood Hills. As he pulls into his driveway, he is shocked to see that his house has been burned to the ground. His wife and children are nowhere to be seen.

The actor bolts out of the car, runs next door to the neighbor's house, and knocks frantically on the door. When the neighbor answers, the actor asks hysterically, "Do you know what happened to my house? Where's my family?"

"Oh, my God," cries the neighbor, "it was horrible! Your agent came over, ran inside your house, raped your wife, axed your children, and then torched the whole place."

The actor takes a step backward and stands there, stupefied. "My agent," he says in shocked disbelief, "came to my *house*?"

It is the tail end of the conversation between Moses and God, and Moses says, "Wait a minute. Let me get this straight. *They* get to keep all the oil, and *we* cut off the tip of our *what*?"

One Wednesday afternoon, a fourth-grade teacher announces to her class, "Children, I'm going to ask you a question, and if anyone can answer it correctly, they can take tomorrow off from school."

Of course, this gets the immediate and undivided attention of all the students. They lean forward in their chairs and listen intently.

"All right," says the teacher, "here is the question: How many grains of sand are there on the beach at Coney Island?"

Needless to say, none of the children knows the answer.

The following day, the teacher says, "If you can answer *today's* question correctly, you can take tomorrow off from school. The question is: How many drops of water are there in the Hudson River?"

The children sit in silence, frustrated by this second impossibly difficult question. Dirty Ernie, sitting in the back of the class, is particularly annoyed. "I'm going to fix her," he thinks. That night, he goes home and paints two golf balls black.

Friday, the teacher says, "Okay, here is today's question . . ." But before she can get it out, Dirty Ernie rolls the two painted golf balls to the front of the room. With a loud clatter, the golf balls hit the wall right below the blackboard. Startled, the teacher looks around the room and says, "All right, who's the comedian with the black balls?"

"Eddie Murphy," Ernie replies. "I'll see ya Tuesday."

■▼■

Q: What's the first thing you know?
A: Old Jed's a millionaire.

■▼■

A therapist says to her new patient, "So, you said that you wanted to see me because you keep obsessing about your mother. Can you tell me a little bit about that?"

"Well," says the man, "it started last week. One day I woke up and I started thinking about my mother. I couldn't get her out of my mind, so I called her to see if everything was all right. She said that she was fine, but that didn't help me. I still kept thinking about her all day and all night. Every night now, I lie awake thinking about her. I can't sleep until I go downstairs and eat a piece of dry toast."

The therapist says to him, "Just one piece of dry toast for a *big boy* like *you*?"

Q: What do you call a person who speaks two languages?
A: Bilingual.
Q: What do you call a person who speaks three languages?
A: Trilingual.
Q: What do you call a person who speaks one language?
A: American.

A teacher says to her class, "For our math problem today, I want you to figure out how many seconds there are in a year."

The children get out their paper and pencils and

are just starting to get to work, when a Polish kid in the back raises his hand. The teacher is quite surprised. "Ivan," she says, "do you know the answer already?"

"Yes, I do," replies Ivan. "There are twelve seconds in a year."

"Twelve?" asks the teacher.

"Yep," says Ivan. "January second, February second, March second . . ."

Q: What is it called when a fifteen-year-old girl decides to become a nun?

A: A premature immaculation.

A little boy is visiting his grandmother, and he asks her, "Grandma, how old are you?"

"It's not polite to ask people their age," the grandmother gently chides. "Sometimes people don't like to answer personal questions like that."

"Oh," says the little boy. "Well, then, how much do you weigh?"

"Stop that right now!" replies the grandmother, raising her voice. "I *told* you that it's very impolite to ask personal questions!"

The little boy thinks for a moment, then says, "Grandma, why did Grampa leave you?"

"That's it!" shouts the grandmother. "Go in the other room, RIGHT NOW!"

The little boy goes into the next room and happens to notice that his grandmother's driver's license is on the table. He goes over and studies it very carefully.

After a few minutes, the little boy walks back into the first room and says, "Grandma, I know how old you are, I know how much you weigh, and I know why Grampa left you: you got an F in sex!"

■▼■

I was driving behind a car and I could see two women sitting in the front seat. The woman who was driving had a hairstyle that I can only describe as wild. On the back of the car there was a bumper sticker that read, "My only domestic quality is that I live in a house."

■▼■

An eighty-year-old woman goes to the doctor and finds out, much to her great surprise, that she is pregnant. She immediately calls her husband on the telephone. "You old coot," she says, "you got me pregnant."

The husband pauses for a moment, then asks, "Who *is* this?"

■▼■

A Polish man is staying at a hotel in New York on vacation and he's talking to the bellman. The bellman notices that the man seems to have a sense of humor, so he decides to tell the visitor a joke. "Okay," says the bellman, "I've got a riddle for you."

"Oh, great," says the Pole. "I love riddles."

So the bellman continues. "All right," he says, "here goes: I am my father's son but I'm not my brother. Who am I?"

The Polish man scratches his head and thinks for a moment. Finally he says, "I don't know. Who are you?"

"I'm me!" says the bellman.

"Oh, right!" says the Pole, "right! Say, that's pretty good!"

After his vacation, the Polish man returns to his home in Poland. One night shortly after he has gotten back, he is sitting around with some of his friends. "I heard a very good riddle when I was in America," he says. "See if you can figure this out: I am my father's son but I'm not my brother. Who am I?"

His friends look around at each other, but nobody can come up with the answer. Finally one of the friends says, "I don't know. Who are you?"

And the Polish man says, "Well, strange as it may seem, I'm the bellman in a New York hotel!"

Q: What's the difference between a lawyer and a vulture?
A: Frequent-flyer miles.

Q: What are the three different types of sex?

A: Living-room sex, bedroom sex, and hallway sex. Living-room sex is the wild kind of sex you have at the beginning of a relationship, where you're screwing in every room of the house, including the living room. Bedroom sex is the kind of sex you have after five years of marriage, where you mostly just do it in the bedroom. Hallway sex is when you've been together too long after the relationship has gone sour, and the only contact you have with one another is when you pass in the hallway and say, "Fuck you," to each other.

■■■

The artist formerly known as Prince: proof that Jimi Hendrix actually *did* screw Liberace.

■■■

From a very early age, Rusty had always been very interested in science. Every year in school, he made straight A's in the subject. When he began his junior year in high school, he begged his parents to buy him his very own chemistry set. This went on for several months until Christmas. When Rusty opened his presents, he found that his wish had come true, and immediately he ran downstairs to the basement to begin setting up his lab.

A few hours later, his father went down to see

how Rusty was doing. He found him, surrounded by test tubes, pounding at the wall with a hammer.

"Son," asked the father, "why are you pounding that nail into the wall?"

"This isn't a nail, Dad," Rusty replied, "it's actually a worm. You see," he continued, holding up a test tube, "I soaked him in this special mixture that I just made."

The father's eyes lit up. "I'll make you a deal, pal," he said to his son. "If you lend me that test tube, I'll buy you a brand-new Ford!"

Rusty was only too glad to hand it over.

The next day, however, when Rusty got home from school he was surprised to see a brand-new red Mercedes in the driveway. "Hey, Dad," he called, running into the house, "what's up?"

"The Ford's in the garage," explained the father, "and the Mercedes is from your Mother."

■▼■

Q: What do a cobra and a two-inch penis have in common?
A: No one wants to fuck with either of them.

■▼■

It is late one night during the Reagan presidency, and Ronald can't sleep, so he decides to take a walk through the portrait gallery at the White House. He stops in front of Washington's portrait and says, "George, you were the father of our country. What can I do to best help our country in these trying times?"

Suddenly, out of the portrait, a white mist appears. Reagan is startled and then completely amazed as the mist coalesces into the ghost of George Washington. The ghost looks down at Reagan and says, "Go to the Congress!"

A somewhat spooked Reagan walks farther down the hall and stops in front of Jefferson's portrait. "Tom," says Reagan, still not quite believing this is all actually happening to him, "how can I best help this country in these trying times?"

Jefferson's ghost appears out of the painting and says, "Go to the people!"

Now Reagan is getting quite excited to be talking to these great men, so he walks a little farther down the hall. When he comes to Lincoln's portrait, he says, "Abe, please appear to me and tell me how I can best help the country in these trying times?"

Lincoln's ghost emerges from the portrait and says, "Go to the theater!"

Q: How do crazy people go through the forest?
A: They take the psycho path.

A new building is being erected directly next door to a convent. More annoying to the sisters than the constant din of the jackhammers, drills, and power saws are the loud curses and extremely foul language thrown about by the construction workers.

After several days of their prayers being interrupted by the constant barrage of profanity, the Mother Superior angrily storms over to the construction site and demands to see the foreman. After enduring her diatribe, the foreman says, "I'm sorry, Sister, but we believe in calling a spade a spade."

"The heck you do," replies the Mother Superior, "you call it a fucking shovel!"

A man walks up to a lady on the street and asks, "Can I paint you in the nude?"

She replies, "I'm not a model."

He says, "I'm not a painter."

∎∎∎

Sister Agatha asks her third-grade class what they want to be when they grow up. Susan says, "I'd like to be a nurse."

Next, Jeremy says, "I want to be a fireman."

Betty says, "I'm going to be a prostitute."

Sister Agatha falls to the floor in a dead faint. When she regains consciousness, she asks again what Betty said.

Betty repeats, "I'm going to be a prostitute."

A peaceful smile breaks out on Sister Agatha's face. "Thanks be to God," says the nun. "I thought you said 'a Protestant.'"

∎∎∎

They did a survey of gays and discovered that in twenty percent of the cases, their homosexuality was hereditary. The other eighty percent were sucked into it.

∎∎∎

To the astonishment of the entire world, Elvis is revealed to still be alive. His managers announce that he will perform his first comeback concert at a dinner theater in New Jersey. Tickets sell out in twenty minutes, and on the night of the concert, the atmosphere in the small theater is positively electric. About ten minutes after all the meals have been served, the lights dim. A loud roar goes up from the audience, and when the M.C. announces Elvis's name, the place breaks out in complete pandemonium.

The band starts blasting away, a spotlight hits the curtain at the side of the stage, and into the light walks Elvis. But this is like no Elvis we've ever seen before. Elvis has gotten huge. He is enormous. Fatter than any of the photos ever seen of him. He's so fat that the watches he's wearing on each wrist are in different time zones. He waddles out onto the stage. When he hits center stage, the band finishes a loud fanfare and then breaks into "Love Me Tender."

The crowd goes crazy as Elvis begins to sing this great hit. In the middle of the song Elvis tells the band to bring it down, and they immediately drop the volume. They are playing quietly as Elvis walks to the front of the stage, obviously about to speak. The crowd falls to a hush. Elvis looks straight at a middle-aged woman sitting at a table right down in front, and says, "Hey, baby, do you love your Elvis?"

"Oh yes!" she screams. "I love my Elvis!"

"You know I'm the king, don't ya', baby?" he murmurs.

She shouts, "You're the king! You're the king!"

"Would you do anything for Elvis?" he asks as he inches closer to her.

"I'd do anything for you, Elvis, *anything*!"

He slowly gets down on one knee and says, "Anything, baby?"

"Yes, Elvis," the woman shrieks, tears streaming down her face, "you know I would!"

"Baby," says Elvis as his voice drops almost to a whisper, "we're talking *anything*."

"Yes, I'd do anything for you, Elvis! You're the king! You're the king!"

"Baby," says Elvis, "you gonna eat that baked potato?"

▼▼▼

Q: What do you get when you cross Arnold Schwarzenegger and a Jewish guy?

A: You get Conan the Distributor.

▼▼▼

A Jewish man is lying on his deathbed, and the end seems to be very near. He turns to his small son, who is standing by the bedside, and whispers, "I think I'm going to die now." The man stops, takes a deep breath, and continues, "Before I go, all I want is to have just one more taste of your mother's chopped liver." He stops, coughs, and then gasps, "It's downstairs on the top shelf of the refrigerator. Get it quickly and please put some on my tongue before I go!"

The little boy runs lickety-split down the stairs. The man is gasping for breath as the son bursts back into the room. The man opens his mouth and sticks out his trembling tongue. The boy tells him, "Mom says it's for *after*."

Q: How many female singers does it take to change a lightbulb?

A: Just one to get up on the ladder, and then the rest of the room revolves around her.

Three guys are talking about bars in their respective hometowns. The first guy, an Irish man, proudly boasts, "Up in Boston, we've got this place called Paddy's. If you go into Paddy's and buy your first drink, then buy a second, Paddy will give you the third drink on the house!"

The next guy, an Italian from New York, says, "Well, in Brooklyn we've got this place called Vinnie's. Now, if you go into Vinnie's and buy two or three drinks, Vinnie will let you drink the rest of the night for free!"

The third guy, a Polish man, says, "Well, in Chicago, we've got this place called Bob's. When you go into Bob's, you get your first drink for free, your second drink free, your third drink free, and then a bunch of guys take you into the back room and get you *laid*. All for free!"

"Wow!" says the Irish guy. "That's really remarkable!"

The guy from New York says, "Yeah! That's incredible! Did that actually *happen* to you?"

"Well," replies the Polish guy, "it didn't happen to me *personally*, but it happened to my *sister*!"

***

Q: Did you hear about the Polish coyote?
A: He chewed off three legs and was *still* caught in the trap.

***

A Polish man is sitting in a restaurant when all of a sudden a woman at the table next to him begins to choke on her food. It gets lodged in her throat so that she can't breathe, and she starts gasping for air. The people at her table all start to panic and don't know what to do, and the woman starts to turn blue.

Suddenly, the Polish man leaps from his chair, runs over to the woman, pulls up her dress, yanks down her underwear, and starts running his tongue all over her bare butt. The woman is so shocked by this that she swallows really hard and her food goes right down.

The woman starts breathing again, and the people at her table all start to cheer. Then the friends crowd around the Polish man. "You saved her!" they cry with joy. "You saved her life! How did you know so quickly what to do?" they ask.

"Aw," replies the Polish guy modestly, "that heinie-lick maneuver works every time."

Q: What do you find inside a clean nose?
A: Fingerprints.

An actor calls up his agent and says, "Hello, is Sid there?"

The secretary says, "Oh, I'm sorry, uh, but you see, Sid passed away last Friday."

"Oh," says the actor, "thanks," and he hangs up.

Ten minutes later he calls back and says, "Hi, can I speak to Sid?"

"Well, I think I just spoke to you," says the secretary, "and I told you that Sid died last week."

"Oh," says the actor.

Five minutes later, the actor calls back and says, "Is Sid in?"

At this point the secretary explodes. "Look," she says angrily into the telephone, "I recognize your voice. You called twice before and I told you that Sid is DEAD! What do you keep calling for?"

"Well," says the actor, "I just love to hear you say it."

A Hollywood agent is walking down the street and he accidentally steps in dog shit. He looks down at his foot and cries out in distress, "I'm melting!"

■◆■

One day out in Los Angeles an actor bursts into his agent's office and pulls out a gun. The actor's hand is trembling, his face is all red, and he is sweating profusely. As he holds the wobbling gun trained on the agent, he says, "All right, I've had it. You sent me over to ABC for that fucking sitcom and it was a goddamn *joke*!"

"W-w-what do you mean?" stammers the agent.

The actor can hardly speak through his rage. "They gave me the job, we were in rehearsal, and then that prick bastard, Bob Kline, that asshole head of ABC, wrote my part out of the show!" The actor now places the muzzle of the gun firmly onto the forehead of the agent.

"I'm going over to ABC right now," says the actor, his voice trembling with anger, "and I'm gonna blow that motherfucker Bob Kline away!" The agent swallows hard as the actor says, "I'd kill *you* right now, but it would just be a waste of good bullets."

With that, the actor rushes out of the agent's office.

The agent immediately picks up the phone and dials ABC.

"Bob Kline's office," answers the secretary.

"This is Sid Gert over at CAA," says the agent. "I need to speak to Bob Kline! Quickly!"

The secretary politely replies, "I'm sorry, Mr. Gert, but Mr. Kline is in a meeting."

"I need to speak to Bob Kline right now!" gasps the agent.

"I'm sorry, Mr. Gert," replies the secretary calmly, "but Mr. Kline left strict instructions not to be disturbed."

"But this," cries Sid, "is an emergency!"

Eventually Sid is put through. The head of ABC picks up the phone and says, "Hello, this is Bob Kline."

"Bob!" says the agent, "this is Sid Gert from CAA! Right now a client of mine is on his way over there. He's got a gun and he says he's going to kill you! But that's not why I called . . ."

One night I had just broken up with a girlfriend, and I was feeling a little depressed. A man about the same age as me got into my cab, and I decided to talk to him about the way I was feeling. This led to a very interesting discussion about relationships. Finally, the man said to me, "Well, there are a lot of women out there. You never know when someone will walk around the corner and it will be your next ex-lover!"

Q: Why do you fuck sheep on the edge of a cliff?
A: They push back harder.

■▼■

A woman says to her husband, "Honey, I tried to turn that lamp on and it didn't work. Could you take a look at it?"

The husband sarcastically replies, "Do I look like an electrician?"

The next day the woman is doing the dishes and she says to her husband, "Honey, could you do something about this drain? It's starting to get stopped up."

The husband sneers, "Do I look like a plumber?"

The following day, a little boy from the neighborhood hits a baseball through one of their windows. "Honey," says the woman to the husband, "you had better fix this window."

The husband scoffs, "Do I look like a glazier?"

When the husband comes home on the fourth day, everything is working. The lamp is shining brightly, the drain is unclogged, and the window has been replaced. He can't believe it. He says to his wife, "Hey, what happened?"

The wife answers, "Oh, the superintendent took care of it."

"That's great!" says the husband. "What did he charge us?"

"Nothing."

"He did all this work for nothing?" asks the husband. "Didn't he want *something*?"

"Well, he gave me a choice," explains the wife. "He said that I could either bake him a cake or screw him."

"So what kind of cake did you make?" the husband asks.

The wife says, "Do I look like a baker?"

■■■

These two very old English gentlemen meet in their exclusive club in London. Over tea, the first man tells the other one, "Last year I went on a safari to Africa."

"Oh, really?" says the second old gentleman. "Did you have a good time?"

"Yes," replies the first man, "it was wonderful. We went lion hunting. I remember at one point we were walking along the veldt area, I had my gun at the ready, and then we came upon this huge out-cropping of rocks. I looked up, and up on top of the rocks I saw this huge lion ready to pounce. I went AAAGH! Well, I tell you, I just shit my pants!"

The other gentleman says, "Well, yes, that's quite understandable. I probably would have done the exact same thing under the same circumstances."

"No, no, no," says the first man. "You don't understand. Not *then*! I did it just *now* when I went AAAGH!"

■▼■

Q: How can you tell when a blonde has been making chocolate-chip cookies in your kitchen?
A: You find M&M shells all over the floor.

■▼■

A very unusual situation arises at the most exclusive hotel in town. An Indian gentleman, the Maharaji of Sharma, has checked into the grand suite. They are giving him the finest treatment and tremendous attention. At the end of the first week, he calls down to the front desk to order breakfast. "This is the Maharaji of Sharma, and I would like to order my breakfast for the morning."

The receptionist politely replies, "Yes, sir. You're a very special guest here at the hotel, and we hope you're enjoying your stay here with us. Whatever you would like to have, just say the word and it's yours."

"All right," says the Maharaji, "I'll get right to the order. What I would like to have for breakfast this morning is two pieces of toast. One piece of toast should be very dark—black, breaking up as you put it on the plate. The other piece of toast should be almost raw. You know what I mean by raw toast? It should look like it did not touch the toaster."

The receptionist says to him, "I've never had an order quite like this."

"Yes," replies the Maharaji. "But this is exactly what I want. Next I would like to have two eggs. Bull's-eye eggs. You know what I mean, bull's-eye eggs? Good. But one of the eggs should be cold, cold as a witch's tit, and the other egg, the yolk should be splattered across the white in a very peculiar kind of pattern."

"Well," says the receptionist, "we're certainly going to do our best to please you with your order. . . ."

The Maharaji continues, "Now I would like to get on to the bacon. I know that you serve bacon because you're not strictly kosher here. I would like to have two pieces of bacon. One piece should be to match the toast, black. The other piece of the bacon should be practically raw."

"Yes, sir, that will be two pieces of bacon—"

"And to conclude this order," says the Maharaji, "I would like to have a cup of coffee."

The receptionist repeats, "A cup of coffee, yes, sir—"

"Just a second," interrupts the Maharaji, "I want to give you the temperature of the coffee. I want it to be lukewarm."

"This is very unusual," says the receptionist. "We have *hot* coffee and we can serve you *iced* coffee on the side, if you wish. Any way that you would like it."

The Maharaji replies, "If I wanted hot or iced, I

would have asked for it that way. No. I want it luke-warm."

The receptionist says to the Maharaji, "I think I have this order straight, sir. I'm not going to bore you by reading it back to you, but I must tell you, Maharaji, that as much as we wish to please you, this is a very unusual order. I'm not sure if we're going to be able to deliver this."

"I don't know why not," says the Maharaji. "I've gotten this order every day this week, and I didn't even order it!"

■■■

Q: Why do some men give names to their penises?
A: They want to be on a first-name basis with the one that makes all their decisions for them.

■■■

A barber opens up a new shop in a small town. The first day he is open, a minister comes in. When the haircut is finished, the minister asks the barber how much he owes him. "Oh," replies the barber, "I never charge a man who does God's work."

The next morning when the barber arrives at his shop, he finds three loaves of freshly baked bread on the doorstep, with a kind note of thanks from the minister. Later that day, a priest comes into the shop.

The barber gives the priest a nice haircut, and when it's done, the priest inquires as to the amount of the bill. The barber tells him, "I never charge a man of the cloth."

The next morning, the barber finds three bottles of wine on the doorstep with a nice note from the priest. Near the end of the day, a rabbi comes into his barbershop. The barber gives him a haircut, and when he's done, the rabbi asks, "So, how much do I owe you?"

The barber bows politely and says, "I never charge a man who works for the Lord."

The following morning, on his front doorstep, the barber finds three rabbis.

Q: What do a condom and a trombone player have in common?
A: Sometimes you have to use one, but it really feels better without it.

A guy is having sex with a woman, and he gets her in a position where her legs are up in front of his chest. As he makes love to her, he notices that the toes on both of her feet begin to curl up, then straighten out. Odder still, when he moves faster, her toes curl up and straighten out faster. Then, when he slows down again, her toes move slower again.

The guy has never seen this kind of reaction

before, so when they are done, he asks the woman, "Was it okay? Did you enjoy it?"

"Uh . . . yes," answers the woman. "You're quite good."

The man, reassured, then inquires, "Well, would you like to do it again?"

"Sure," replies the woman, "but this time, could I first take off my panty hose?"

■▰▰

Q: How can you distinguish the different clans in Scotland?

A: If there's a quarter-pounder under his kilt, he's a MacDonald.

■▰▰

A guy goes into a bar, sits down, and sees a beautiful creature sitting at the other end of the bar. He calls the bartender over and says, "Bring me a whiskey, and buy that woman a drink."

The bartender tells him, "Listen, pal. Save your money. She's a lesbian."

"A lesbian?" says the guy. "It doesn't matter. Buy her a drink."

The bartender brings the guy his whiskey and then gets a drink for the woman. Upon receiving her drink, the woman looks over at the man, takes a sip, nods her thanks, and then looks away, returning to her drink.

The man calls the bartender over and orders, "Buy her another drink! Whatever she wants!"

"I'm telling you," the bartender tries to explain, "you're wasting your money. She's a lesbian."

The man insists, and so the bartender gets the woman another drink. She nods her thanks to the guy, but that's it.

This happens five or six more times, but the woman just sits over at the other end of the bar, minding her own business. By now, though, the guy is getting pretty looped, so he goes over to the woman and slurs, "Excuse me, can I ask you something?"

The woman replies, "Sure."

"So tell me," says the man, "where are you from in Lesbia?"

Q: What do a bass solo and premature ejaculation have in common?

A: With both of them, you can see it coming, but there's not a damn thing you can do about it.

A young gunfighter rides into Dodge City. He gallops up to the largest saloon he sees and dismounts. As soon as he walks through the swinging doors, he is met with the lively music of a tinkling piano and sees some beautiful women dancing on the stage. He is absolutely awestruck, though, to see the famous Doc Holliday playing poker at one of the tables.

The gunfighter strolls right over to the legendary man, who is at that moment looking at his cards. "Excuse me," he says, "but are you Doc Holliday, friend to gunfighter and lawman alike?"

Doc Holliday slowly puts his cards down and says, "Why, yes I am. Are you going to start trouble?"

"No, no!" says the gunfighter, holding up his hands. "I was just wondering if you could critique my shooting style."

Doc Holliday relaxes, smiles, and replies, "Sure, son, I'd be happy to."

In a split second, the Colt .45 comes out of the young man's holster and he gets off a shot. The bullet blows the cuff link off of the piano player's right sleeve. The piano player, meanwhile, doesn't even miss a beat. He just keeps on playing, the dancing girls keep dancing, and the people in the saloon just keep on drinking and playing cards.

The gunfighter twirls the gun and then smoothly slips it back into its holster. A split second goes by and out comes the gun again. He blasts off a second shot, and this one shoots the cuff link off of the piano player's left sleeve. The cuff link makes an arc through the air and then clatters to the floor at the feet of Doc Holliday. The piano player doesn't miss a beat, though, and just keeps playing away. The dancing girls are still doing the cancan, people keep on drinking, and the gambling wheels still keep spinning.

Doc Holliday looks up at the kid and says, "That's some mighty fancy shooting there, young man."

"Thank you, sir," replies the kid.

"However, I have *two* suggestions for you," says Doc Holliday.

The gunfighter eagerly asks, "Oh, yeah? Please tell me!"

"Well," says Doc, rolling himself a cigarette, "I noticed on your first shot that there was a slight hesitation on your equipment, and I think there might be a little burr on the hammer of your gun. Go down the street here, to Al's Gunsmith shop, and ask Al to file that off for you."

The kid says, "Great! Thanks! What's the second suggestion?"

"When you get finished in Al's," answers Doc Holliday as he lights up his cigarette, "go across the street to the general store. Ask Fred in the general store to dip your *entire* gun in bear grease."

"Bear grease!" the kid exclaims. "Why?"

"Because," replies Doc, letting out a puff of smoke, "when Wyatt finishes playing this tune, he's gonna shove that gun up your ass."

■▾■

Q: What's the best thing about being gay?
A: After sex, you have someone intelligent to talk to.

■▾■

An Englishman, an American, and a Polish guy are all about to be executed by a firing squad. The Englishman is called up first. After he smokes his last cigarette, the rifles are raised up and aimed directly at his heart. He hears the commanding officer shout, "Ready . . . Aim . . ."

Thinking fast, the Englishman cries out, "TORNADO!" All the soldiers quickly scramble for cover, and the Englishman slips away and escapes.

The American is chosen to be next, and after refusing the blindfold, he watches in horror as the guns bear down on him. The commanding officer shouts, "Ready . . . Aim . . ."

Thinking on his feet, the American suddenly screams, "HURRICANE!" The soldiers all duck for cover and the American gets away.

Finally, the Polish guy gets dragged up in front of the bullet-ridden wall. He can't think of anything for his last request, and is still scratching his head as the rifles draw a bead right between his eyes. The commanding officer quickly gives the orders, "Ready . . . Aim . . ."

The Polish guy suddenly yells, "FIRE!"

Q: Did you hear what happened to the couple who accidentally switched their K-Y jelly with putty?
A: All their windows fell out.

A woman once asked me if I knew what the three different types of orgasms are. When I said that I didn't, she explained them to me. "First," she said, "is the religious orgasm: 'Oh God! *Oh God! OH GOD!*' Then there is the positive orgasm: 'Oh yes! *Oh yes! OH YES!*' And the third type of orgasm is the fake orgasm: 'Oh Jim! *Oh Jim! OH JIM!*'"

A man asks his wife what she wants for her birthday. She replies, "I want a divorce."

The man replies, "Gee, I wasn't planning on spending that much."

❖❖❖

A man living in a nudist camp gets a letter from his mother requesting that he send her a photo of himself. Unfortunately, the only pictures he has are ones in which he is wearing no clothes. So he cuts a snapshot in half, then sends the photo showing him from the waist up to his mother.

His mother is so pleased with the picture that she asks him to send one to his grandmother. The man thinks to himself, "Grandma's eyesight is so bad these days, I'll just send her the bottom half."

A week later he receives a letter from his grandmother. In the letter she writes, "I liked your picture, but your new hairstyle makes your nose look too long."

❖❖❖

A violinist is playing on the street for change when suddenly he hears a noise behind him. He looks around and sees two dogs screwing in the alley. "Don't just stand there," growls one of the dogs, "play 'Bolero'!"

❖❖❖

Two men appearing to be in their early thirties got into my taxi. One of them was wearing a fedora hat and had a handlebar mustache that curled around at the ends. I told them a joke that they really liked, and then I asked them what kind of work they did. The man with the hat told me that he worked as a translator.

When Japanese businessmen come to New York, this man gives them a tour of the city, and teaches them the local customs and how to get around. "Tell me," I said, "I've heard that the Japanese don't have much of a sense of humor. Is that true?"

"Well, they do," he replied, "but it's just very different from ours. If you translated a Japanese joke into English, you wouldn't get it. Even if you understood every word, the humor just wouldn't translate. The same would be true the other way around. If you tried telling a Japanese person an English joke, they wouldn't understand what was funny about it. Actually, that reminds me of a true story."

The man went on to tell me this story:

"I was living in Japan with my parents about twenty-five years ago, and I met an American man in a nightclub. This was the most popular club in Tokyo, and the American worked as the M.C. for the shows. The club presented entertainers from all over the world, and one night the headliner was Sammy Davis, Jr.

"Before the show, Mr. Davis asked to speak with the M.C. in his dressing room. When the man got to the dressing room, Sammy explained to him that he was going to warm the audience up with a joke. He then

told the American that he wanted him to translate it into Japanese.

"'Well, I don't recommend that you do that,' said the M.C. 'You see, they won't be able to understand the humor.'

"'No, no,' said Mr. Davis, 'this is a really good joke. They'll love it.'

"'But the humor just doesn't translate over here,' replied the M.C., trying to be as helpful as he could.

"But Sammy would have none of it. 'It'll go over great,' he said. 'You'll see.'

"As the M.C. went out onto the stage, he was sweating bullets. If Mr. Davis told the joke, he knew that it would fall flat and start the whole performance off on the wrong foot. If the show was a flop because of it, the man was very nervous about keeping his job at the club.

"He introduced Sammy Davis, Jr., to the Japanese audience (in Japanese, of course) to thunderous applause. Right away, Sammy began to tell the joke. He said a few lines, then paused and looked at the M.C., waiting for him to translate.

"In his best inner-city dialect, the M.C. began speaking to the audience in Japanese. 'Ladies and gentlemen,' he said, 'Sammy Davis is now telling a joke and I'm supposed to be translating it. I know, though, that the humor is so different that it won't translate, and it won't be funny to you.'

"He paused while Sammy told a few more lines of the joke. He then went on in Japanese. 'I'm really worried. If he doesn't get a laugh, I might be in trouble and lose my job.'

"*Another pause while Sammy told a few more lines.*

"'*I really need your help,*' *said the M.C. to the audience.* '*When he comes to the punch line, I will count to three, and I want you all to start laughing.*'

As the audience began to realize what was happening, some of the people began to chuckle. Hearing this, Sammy was encouraged, thinking he was going over great. With mounting enthusiasm, Sammy Davis got to the end of the joke and hit the punch line. The M.C. counted to three and the audience went wild with hysterical laughter.

"*After the show, Sammy went up to the M.C., patted him on the back, and said, '*You see, kid? I knew you could do it!'"

■■▶

A comedian from New York returns to his hotel late one night after performing at a small comedy club in the Midwest. He steps into the elevator, and just as the doors are closing, a woman in a low-cut dress quickly gets in with him. In the sexiest voice imaginable, she says to the comedian, "I just have to tell you that I think that a sense of humor is *incredibly* sexy! I saw you perform tonight, and you were so funny that you got me really turned on. I'm so hot for you right now that I want to take you up to your hotel room, lick you from head to toe, and then fuck your brains out."

"Wow!" says the comedian. "Did you see the *first* show or the *second* show?"

Q: How do you find an old man in the dark?
A: It ain't hard.

▗▖▖

Two cabdrivers get fed up with their garage. They can't stand dealing with the asshole dispatcher, and worse yet, the greedy owner keeps raising the lease fees. So they decide to quit driving taxis and become chauffeurs. After several years of being in private employ, they meet one evening for a drink.

One of the drivers says to the other, "So tell me, how are you doing?"

"I've been doing pretty good," says the second driver. "I'm working for these people, the Smiths, for the last four years. I drive this big Lincoln Continental, they give me a really big salary, I've got a nice place to live, and I get off Christmas, New Year's, Thanksgiving, and Easter. I'm really happy with my life these days. How are *you* doing?"

The first guy says, "Well, I'm working for these people, the Schwartzes. I drive a big Cadillac, I've got a nice place to live, I make a lot of money, and I get off on this holiday called roshe hosh shannah, this holiday called yome kipper, this holiday called paysak, and this holiday called sukas."

The second guy says, "What kind of jive is this, man? What are these holidays all about? Like, what's this 'sukas'?"

"Well," replies the first guy, "that's when they put up all kinds of trees and stuff."

The second guy says, "Oh, yeah? What about that 'paysak'?"

"They don't eat no bread on that day," explains the first guy, "but I go in the kitchen and the cook gives me whatever I want."

"Yeah?" says the second guy, "well, what about that 'yome kipper'?"

"They don't eat nothin' at all on that day. But I go into the kitchen and eat whatever I want."

"Hmm," says the other guy, "how about that 'roshe hosh shannah'?"

"Oh, man," exclaims the first driver, "that's the best one of all, man. That's when they blow the shofar."

■▪▪

A doctor calls his patient to give him the results of his test. "I have some bad news and some worse news," says the doctor. "The bad news is that you only have twenty-four hours to live."

"Oh, no," says the patient. "What could possibly be worse than that?"

The doctor answers, "Well, I've been trying to reach you since yesterday."

■▪▪

Q: How do Catholics make extra money on hot summer days?
A: They freeze holy water and sell it as Popesicals.

■▪▪

Warren Beatty and the Pope both happen to die on the same day. Because of a heavenly clerical error, the Pope is sent to hell and Warren Beatty goes to heaven. As soon as the Pope arrives in hell, he realizes that there has been a mistake and demands to see the demon in charge. He is immediately brought before the Devil.

"There must be some mistake!" exclaims the Pope. "I'm the Pope! I should be in heaven!"

"Just a moment," says the Devil, "let me get your file up on the computer." A microsecond later, the Devil is looking at the Pope's records. "Hmmm," he says, "you're right. Our apologies. We'll correct the error immediately."

In a split second, the Pope whooshes up to heaven and lands on a fluffy white cloud. As he starts walking in through the Pearly Gates, he sees Warren Beatty walking out. "I'm sorry to do this to you, my son," says the sympathetic pontiff, "but I've been waiting my whole life to kneel at the feet of the Holy Virgin Mary."

Warren Beatty smiles and shrugs his shoulders. "Sorry, padre," he says, "too late."

■▼■

Q: What do you call a person who is fifty percent Latino?
A: Sorta Rican.

■▼■

Out in the Wild West, Jesse James's gang forces a train to stop, and Jesse climbs on board. He bursts into a passenger car, pulls out his guns, and fires. Blam! Blam! "All right!" he yells. "I'm going to fuck all the men and kill all the women!" Blam! Blam! "That's right!" he growls. "I'm going to fuck all the men and kill all the women!"

A guy in the front row says, "Uh, Mr. James, I think you've got it backwards."

Suddenly a high-pitched man's voice in the back calls out, "Excuse me, but *Mr. James* is robbing the train."

Q: You are in a room with a mass murderer, a terrorist, and a lawyer. All you have is a gun with two bullets in it. What do you do?
A: Shoot the lawyer twice.

One afternoon during a weekend workshop, two psychiatrists are having lunch together. One of them says, "Could you please pass me a fuck—I mean *fork*."

The other psychiatrist says, "Do you know what you just did?"

"What?" asks the first man. "I said 'fuck' instead of 'fork.' I'm sorry."

"Yeah," says the second man, "but that was quite a Freudian slip."

"You know," says the first psychiatrist, "it's really weird, but that's my second Freudian slip today. This morning I was having breakfast with my mother, and what I meant to say to her was, 'Please pass the salt,' but the way it came out was, 'You bitch, you ruined my life!'"

Q: What's the definition of mixed emotions?
A: Seeing your mother-in-law driving off a cliff in your brand-new Porsche.

On a crowded airliner a five-year-old boy is throwing a wild temper tantrum. No matter what his frustrated, embarrassed mother does to try to calm him down, the boy continues to scream furiously and kick the seats around him.

Suddenly, from the rear of the plane, an elderly minister slowly walks forward up the aisle. Stopping the flustered mother with an upraised hand, the minister leans down and whispers something into the boy's ear. Instantly, the boy calms down, gently takes his mother's hand, and quietly fastens his seat belt.

All the other passengers burst into spontaneous applause. As the minister slowly makes his way back to his seat, one of the stewardesses takes him by the sleeve. "Excuse me, Reverend," she says quietly, "but what magic words did you use on that little boy?"

The old man smiles serenely and gently says, "I told him that if he didn't cut that shit out, I'd kick his fucking ass to the moon."

■▼■

Q: Where can you get a good cheddar in Israel?
A: Cheeses of Nazareth.

■▼■

A little girl accidentally walks in on her father going to the bathroom. Shocked, she runs to her mother and cries, "Mommy, Mommy! Daddy has a big fat ugly worm hanging out of his wee-wee!"

"That's not a worm, sweetie," comforts the mother, "that's a very important part of Daddy's body. If Daddy didn't have one of those, you wouldn't be here. And now that I think about it . . . neither would I."

■▼■

Q: How do you make paper dolls?
A: Screw an old bag.

■▼■

The international scientific community comes up with an innovative experimental project. They decide to put all of the greatest minds in research together for three full weeks. They set them up in a research facility with everything they need, including state-of-the-art laboratories and the most advanced high-tech equipment available.

This project is an attempt to see what can happen if these scientists are allowed to work together in a positive environment and to freely share ideas in the spirit of international cooperation.

After the second week, one of the scientists leaps up from his lab table, holding a test tube high in the air. "Eureka!" he cries. "Eureka! I've found it! THE CURE FOR CANCER!"

Suddenly, the scientist clutches at his chest and falls over. As he hits the floor, the test tube smashes and the fluid spills out all over the floor. The other scientists rush over to their colleague and find him dead of a heart attack. They quickly try to mop up the liquid from the test tube with a cloth, but it is too late. The fluid has evaporated.

They rush over to the scientist's notes, but it is page after page of indecipherable scribbles and no one can understand them. The scientists all begin to wail and moan. "Oh no! This is terrible! We had it!! We had the cure for cancer! And now it's lost! *Oh no!*"

The director of the program is in the next room and hears all the commotion. He rushes in and says, "What happened? What's the matter?"

Some of the scientists are openly weeping, others are pounding the tables, and some are lying on the floor groaning.

"What is it? What is it?" asks the director.

One of the scientists looks up from the floor and

sobs, "*We had it! We had the cure for cancer, and then we lost it. This is terrible! This is just awful!*"

"Hey, hey, hey! Calm down now," says the director. "Just relax. I mean, we're not making *movies* here."

❖❖❖

Q: Why don't Jewish girls swallow when they give their boyfriends blow jobs?

A: They want to be the spitting images of their mothers.

❖❖❖

An avid golfer gets married, and on his wedding night he makes passionate love to his bride. When they are finished, he reaches over and picks up the telephone. His bride looks at him and asks, "What are you doing, honey?"

"I'm calling room service," he replies. "I thought I'd order up some champagne and some food."

The woman snuggles up to her new husband and says, "Did I ever tell you about the time I had an affair with Jack Nicklaus?"

The man's eyes light up. "You had an affair with Jack Nicklaus?" he exclaims.

"Mmm-hmm," coos the wife. "And *he* didn't make love to me only one time, and then call for room service."

"Oh, well, then . . ." says the husband, a sly smile

crossing his face as he puts down the phone. He then proceeds to make wild love to his bride for the second time. When they're done, though, he is feeling quite tired and very hungry, so he reaches for the phone again.

"What are you doing, sweetheart?" the wife asks.

"Now I'm really *hungry*," says the man. "I'm going to order room service."

"Jack and I didn't just do it *twice* and then order room service," says the bride, smiling lasciviously.

"Oh," says the groom. He rolls back over toward his wife and starts caressing her. He finally manages to make another attempt, and even though it takes a little longer, the husband makes hot, steamy love to his wife for the third time. When they are finished, though, he feels completely famished.

As he reaches for the phone, his wife puts her hand on his arm and asks, "What are you doing now, dear?"

The exasperated man says, "I'm calling Jack Nicklaus. I want to find out what's par for this hole."

❖❖❖

Hitler goes to his astrologer and asks him, "When am I going to die?"

The astrologer carefully studies the astrological chart on the table in front of him, and then tells Hitler, "You will die on a Jewish holiday."

Hitler is quite surprised. "A Jewish holiday?" he asks. "How can you be so sure?"

The astrologer replies, "*Any* day you die will be a Jewish holiday."

A man once said to me, "Remember, if it's got either tits or tires, it's going to cost you a lot of money and cause you a lot of heartache!"

Q: What's the difference between the Rolling Stones and a Scotsman?

A: The Rolling Stones say, "Hey, you, get offa my cloud!" and a Scotsman says, "Hey, McCloud, get offa my ewe!"

And a variation . . .

A man gets invited to the Playboy mansion in Los Angeles for a party. When he arrives there, the party is in full swing and the place is really jumping. Since the man has never been to the mansion before, he decides to go exploring.

He starts to wander from room to room, when he opens up a door and realizes that he has come upon a very unexpected scene. There, before his eyes, the man sees Hef butt-fucking Dennis Weaver. The man shouts out, "Hey! Hey! Hugh! Hugh! Get offa McCloud!"

Q: What do you call E.T. without any morals?
A: E.Z.

•••

A little seven-year-old boy goes out on Halloween in a pirate costume. He goes up to a house and knocks on the door. An old lady opens it and, looking down at the boy, exclaims, "Oh my, a pirate! And tell me, you cute little pirate, where are your buccaneers?"

"Lady," replies the boy impatiently, "they're right under my buck'n hat."

•••

A reporter is on the street with a camera crew and a microphone. He sees three men walking together and stops them, thinking that they might be good subjects for an interview. One man is from Poland, one is from Russia, and the other is from Israel. He says to them, "Excuse me, I'm doing an interview. Can you tell me your opinion on the current meat shortage?"

The Polish guy says, "What's meat?"

The Russian guy says, "What's opinion?"

The Israeli guy says, "What's 'excuse me'?"

•••

Q: What's the difference between a lawyer and a sperm cell?
A: A sperm cell actually has a one-in-two-hundred-million chance of someday becoming a human.

Q: What's the difference between a blonde and a parrot?

A: A parrot can say "no."

Q: What is the mating call of a blonde?

A: "Boy, am I drunk!"

Q: What is the mating call of a brunette?

A: "Has that drunk blonde left yet?"

A man with rapidly thinning hair goes into his regular barbershop and sits down for his haircut. Looking at the shiny dome of the barber, the man feels a certain kinship and says, "I bet you wish as much as I do that there could be an instant cure for baldness."

The barber looks around, lowers his voice, leans in close to the man, and says, "Actually, I *have* discovered a cure. The best thing to cure baldness is, umm, er, shall we say 'female juices.'"

The guy looks up at the barber and exclaims, "But you're as bald as a cue ball!"

"Yeah," replies the barber, "but you've got to admit, I've got a helluva mustache!"

■ ■ ■

Q: What do you get when you lock a gay guy and a Jewish guy in a closet?
A: They come out with a musical.

■ ■ ■

A band is booked into a club for a gig on a Friday night. One full hour before they are supposed to start playing, the drummer shows up and starts setting up his drums. *[When I've told this joke, some of my musician friends have said, "That's a good joke right there!"]* The club owner rushes over to the drummer with a worried look on his face and asks, "Where's the rest of the band?"

The drummer, in a very calm tone of voice, says to him, "Hey, don't worry. The band will be here. I'm the drummer, and I just like to get to the gig a little early so that I can take my time getting set up. It takes me a little longer, you know, with all the cymbals and drum stands and everything. The band *always* comes in later than me, but they'll be here. Just relax."

Somewhat reassured, the club owner walks away. The drummer finishes setting up in about twenty minutes, and is hanging out in the bar for another ten minutes when the club owner scurries over to him and says, "The band's not here yet! Where are they?"

"Look," replies the drummer, "I told you that they always come in later than me, so it isn't at all unusual for them to not be here yet. Really, once they get here, it'll just take them a few minutes to get set up. Take it easy, now."

This time the club owner walks away feeling quite worried. Another fifteen minutes goes by, then ten minutes, and now the club owner is frantic. He runs over to the drummer and is almost hysterical. "Where's the band?" he cries. *"Where's the band?"*

The drummer shakes his head and replies, "I don't know. Actually, this *is* pretty strange. They've never been *this* late before. I'm starting to get worried now myself. I really don't know what to tell you."

"It's almost time to start!" exclaims the club owner. "I've got to have some music! *You* have to get up there and play!"

"What?" says the drummer. "You want me to get up there and play *all alone*?"

"I have a club full of people here!" the owner says. "I've got to have *something* happening onstage!"

"Well, okay," the drummer replies, somewhat hesitantly. He goes over and hops up onto the stage, sits down behind the drum set, and gets out a pair of brushes. With a flourish, he starts to quietly play on the snare drum with the brushes. After a few minutes, all conversation in the club has dwindled down to complete silence. Everyone has become rapt, listening to the drummer, who is really into a deep groove with the brushes. When he realizes that he has everyone's attention, the drummer starts playing the hi-hat and grooving even harder, throwing in accents on the bass drum and cymbals.

After a few minutes of this, a couple gets out onto the dance floor and starts dancing, just to the rhythms of the solo percussionist. Pretty soon, the drummer has everyone in the entire club out on the dance floor, moving to the incredible swing groove that he's laying down. After a few more minutes, a young couple dances over next to the drummer. The woman says to him, "Do you take requests?"

The drummer, continuing to swing like crazy, shrugs his shoulders and says over the fluttering sound of his brushes, "Yeah, I guess so. What would you like to hear?"

The woman asks, "Could you play 'Raindrops Keep Falling on My Head'?"

"FUCK YOU!" shouts the drummer. *"That's what I've been playing for the last TEN MINUTES!"*

Q: What two words will clear out a men's room quicker than anything?

A: NICE DICK!

■▪▪■

A man walks out into his front yard one morning to pick up the newspaper. As he reaches down for it, he sees that a snail is crawling across the paper. "Oh, gross!" mumbles the man, and he quickly flips the snail off into the bushes.

A year later, the man walks out one morning to pick up his newspaper, and he sees the same snail crawling on the paper.

The snail looks up at the man and says, "What was *that* all about?"

■▪▪■

A maître d' goes over to a middle-aged Jewish couple eating in his restaurant. He asks them, "Is anything all right?"

■▪▪■

A Harvard man and a Yale man are good friends, and one night, after eating dinner in a very swanky restaurant, they decide to make a quick stop in the men's room before going out to hit the town. They go into the rest room together and stand next to each other at the urinals. When they are done, the Yale man goes over to one of the sinks and rinses his hands. The Harvard man, however, just stands to the side waiting for the Yale man to finish.

As they are walking out, the Yale man says to his friend, "At *Yale*, they taught *us* to rinse our hands after we piss."

His friend turns to him and replies, "At *Harvard*, they taught *us* not to piss on our hands."

Q: What's the definition of an economic adviser?
A: Someone who wanted to go into accounting but didn't have the personality.

Two sperm are swimming along after being ejaculated. They are swimming and swimming, and then one of them says to the other, "Say, do you mind if we stop and rest for a minute? I'm getting really tired."

"Sure," replies the other one. So they stop and hang out for a couple of minutes, and then they start to swim again.

A little bit later, the second sperm says, "Do you mind if we stop again? I really need to catch my breath."

"No problem," answers the first. They stop once more, and after pausing for a few minutes the two little sperms resume their journey.

After swimming for a while longer, the first sperm exclaims, "Man! I didn't know that it was such a long trip to the cervix!"

"I know!" replies the second sperm. "We haven't even passed the esophagus yet!"

✺✺✺

Two Polish guys are walking down the street. One of them suddenly stops short and says sadly, "Wow! Look at that dead bird." The other Polish guy looks up in the sky and says, "Where?"

✺✺✺

An American man travels to Mexico on business, and he goes to this little, sleepy, lazy town. He arrives at siesta time, and everyone in the town is lying around in hammocks, leaning against buildings, or sleeping on sidewalks. He sees one man still awake leaning against a building with an umbrella over him and a donkey standing right next to him. The American goes over to the man and says, "Excuse me, Señor. Can you tell me what time it is?"

The man says, "*Sí.*" He grabs his donkey by the balls, squeezes hard, and the donkey rears his head up to the right. The man says, "Eet ees one o'clock."

"Thank you very much," says the American. He then proceeds into town and goes about his business. A few hours later, he comes back and sees the same man standing there. Just out of curiosity, he goes up to the man and says, "Excuse me, Señor. I'm sorry to bother you again, but could you tell me what time it is now?"

The man says, "*Sí*." Once again, the man grabs the donkey by the balls and squeezes. This time the donkey rears his head up to the left and the man says, "Ees four-feefteen."

The American says, "Thank you very much." He walks to his car and is about to drive out of town, but his curiosity gets the better of him. He goes back to the Mexican man a third time and says, "What time is it?"

The man squeezes the donkey's balls and the donkey rears his head straight back and the man says, "Ees four-twenty now."

The gringo says, "Thank you very much, you've been very helpful. But tell me something. How is it that you can tell time by squeezing your donkey's balls?"

"Oh, ees very easy, Señor," says the man. "I squeeze the donkey's balls and he rears hees head to the right, to the left, or een the meedle."

"I see," says the American, "but how can you tell time like that?"

The Mexican says, "As soon as the donkey gets hees damn head out of the way, I can see the clock in the tower across the street."

✦✦✦

A woman from Germany was telling me that cab-drivers in Berlin are really crazy. "In Berlin," she said, "we call a red light 'cabdriver green.' We also say that the cabdrivers in Berlin don't drive fast. They fly deep."

▼▼▼

Two middle-aged gentlemen, Cohen and Ginsberg, meet on a cruise on the *Queen Elizabeth II*, and they discover that they have a lot in common. They are both retired garment-industry executives and have been culture vultures throughout their entire lives. They both love opera, classical music, ballet, painting, sculpture, and all the finest cultural activities our civilization has to offer. When they get to Europe they spend the entire three months together, going to the Hermitage, visiting the Louvre, attending every Balkan festival, and generally taking in everything that is edifying to the refined intellectual spirit.

When they return to New York, Ginsberg says to Cohen, "Now we're back in New York, the cultural capital of the world. Why don't we keep up this friendship? This last three months have been the best time I've ever had in my life. Let's get together and go out sometime!"

They agree to meet, and the next week Ginsberg calls Cohen on the phone. He says, "Cohen, I've got two tickets to the Met for tonight. Placido Domingo is going to be singing *Tosca*. What do you say?"

Cohen replies, "Placido Domingo! *Tosca!* Oh, if only I could! Unfortunately, though, tonight Shapiro is playing."

The following week, Ginsberg gives Cohen another call. He says, "Cohen, I've got two tickets for tomorrow night. The New York Philharmonic. Zubin Mehta is going to be conducting an entire Beethoven program. What do you say?"

"Oh, my," says Cohen, "the New York Philharmonic! Zubin Mehta! Beethoven! Ah! If only I could. It's just that tomorrow night, Shapiro is playing."

Now Ginsberg waits a couple of weeks more, then he calls Cohen again. "Cohen," he says, "tonight I've got two tickets to the Bolshoi. A special appearance by Baryshnikov. Front-row-center seats. What do you say?"

"This is too much," says Cohen. "The Bolshoi, my favorite group! Baryshnikov! Front row center! But I can't make it. Unfortunately, tonight Shapiro is playing."

Ginsberg is astonished and baffled. "Who is Shapiro? What does he play? Where is he playing?"

Cohen replies, "I don't know who Shapiro is, I don't know what he plays, and I don't know where he's playing. All I know is that when Shapiro is playing, I'm shtupping his wife."

Q: How many video editors does it take to change a lightbulb?
A: "I can change it for you, but it's not gonna look any better."

Finkelstein and Greenburg are both addicted to gin rummy, and they happen to meet in the card room at their country club. Coincidentally, this occurs the day after Finkelstein found his wife in bed with Greenburg.

"All right," says Finkelstein, "I know you've been screwing my wife, but I still love her. Let's settle this in a civilized manner. We'll play a game of gin and the winner gets to keep her."

"Okay," replies Greenburg, "but just to make it interesting, let's play for a penny a point."

Q: How does a musician make a million dollars?
A: He starts out with seven million.

A Polish guy is walking down the street and stops a man to ask for the time. The man, looking at his watch, helpfully responds, "Why, certainly! The time is now four o'clock."

The Polish guy scratches his head and says, "You know, it's really weird. I've been asking people that question all day long, and each time I get a different answer."

A man in New York has heard all his life about how the parties in Texas are really wild, so he decides that he's going to check it out for himself. He saves up some money, and when his next vacation comes around, he flies to Houston. On his first night there, he goes to a bar and strikes up a conversation with the man sitting next to him.

"You know," he says, "for years and years I've heard stories about Texas parties. I finally decided to check it out for myself, and I came down here with one—and only one—purpose in mind: to go to some *real* Texas parties."

"How long have you been here?" asks the man at the bar.

The New Yorker replies, "I just got in today."

"Well, you're in luck," says the Texan. "I'm having a party at my place tonight. You're welcome to come along if you like."

"That's fantastic!" exclaims the New Yorker. "I'd *love* to come!"

"But," the man says, "before you agree to come, I should warn you about something. There's probably going to be a whole lot of drinking going on at this party." Then, lowering his voice, the man continues, "And in all likelihood, there will also be some drugs."

"Oh, that's okay," replies the New Yorker. "As a matter of fact, I wouldn't have expected anything less from a Texas party. I'm up for it!"

"Well," says the man, "there's also something else I should warn you about. After the party gets going, there's a good chance that there may actually be some fucking going on."

The New Yorker starts rubbing his hands together. "This is amazing! This is just like what I heard. It sounds fantastic! I'm ready!"

The man leans in close and confides, "Well, there's just one more thing you should know. When the party gets really rocking, there could also be some fighting going on."

"Oh, I understand," says the New Yorker. "Sometimes when a party gets really wild, it can be hard to keep everything under control. So that's no problem for me. I'm ready for *anything*. I want the whole Texas party experience, no matter what happens!"

"Well, then," says the man, getting up off of his bar stool, "let's get going!"

The two men go outside, and as soon as they get into the Texan's pickup truck, the New Yorker suddenly says, "Wait a minute! We're going to a party. I don't know if I'm dressed right. Is what I'm wearing okay?"

"Sure!" exclaims the Texan. "It's just going to be the two of us!"

Q: What does a lawyer use for birth control?
A: His personality.

A young man is trying to hitchhike in Washington, D.C. He is very surprised to find that every time a car pulls over, the driver inside asks him, "Are you a Republican or a Democrat?"

The hitchhiker always replies truthfully, "I'm a Democrat." Upon hearing his response, the drivers immediately hit the gas, squeal their tires, and leave him in a cloud of dust. This happens four or five times, and finally the man begins to get the picture.

The next car that pulls over is a hot-looking convertible with a beautiful blonde woman in the driver's seat. The woman looks at the hitchhiker and asks lasciviously, "Are you a Republican or a Democrat?"

The young man replies eagerly, "I'm a Republican!"

"Get in!" says the woman.

As they begin driving, the man can't keep his eyes off the beautiful blonde. Her long hair is waving in the breeze, and the wind is blowing her blouse open, partially revealing her breasts.

Suddenly the man cries out, "STOP THE CAR! STOP THE CAR!"

The woman slams on the brakes and skids off the side of the road to a sudden stop. "What happened?" she exclaims. "What's the matter?"

The young man, perspiring profusely, replies, "I've only been a Republican for five minutes, and *already* I feel like screwing somebody!"

■■■

René Descartes walks into a bar and sits down. The bartender walks over to him and asks, "Would you like a drink?"

Descartes replies, "I think not," and disappears.

■■■

Q: How was yodeling invented?

A: Back in the olden days, a man was traveling through Switzerland. Nightfall was rapidly approaching, and the man had nowhere to sleep. He went up to a farmhouse and asked the farmer if he could spend the night. The farmer told him that it would be all right, and that he could sleep in the barn. The man went into the barn to bed down, and the farmer went back into the house.

The farmer's daughter came down from upstairs and asked the farmer, "Who was that man going into the barn?"

"That's some fellow traveling through," answered the farmer. "He needed a place to stay for the night, so I said that he could sleep in the barn."

The daughter then asked the farmer, "Did you offer the man anything to eat?"

"Gee, no, I didn't," the farmer answered.

The daughter said, "Well, I'm going to take him some food." She went into the kitchen, prepared a plate of food, and then took it out to the barn. The daughter was in the barn for an hour before returning to the house. When she came back in, her clothes were all disheveled and buttoned up wrong, and she had several strands of straw tangled up in her long blond hair. She immediately went up the stairs to her bedroom and went to sleep.

A little later, the farmer's wife came down and asked the farmer why their daughter went to bed so early. "I don't know," said the farmer. "I told a man that he could sleep in the barn, and our daughter took him some food."

"Oh," replied the wife. "Well, did you offer the man anything to drink?"

"Umm, no, I didn't," said the farmer.

The wife then said, "I'm going to take something out there for him to drink." The wife went to the cellar, got a bottle of wine, then went out to the barn. She did not return for over an hour, and when she came back into the house, her clothes were also messed up, and she had straw twisted into *her* blond hair. She went straight up the stairs and into bed.

The next morning at sunrise, the man in the barn got up and continued on his journey, waving to the farmer as he left the farm.

A few hours later, the daughter woke up and came rushing downstairs. She went right out to the barn, only to find it empty. She ran back into the house. "Where's the man from the barn?" she eagerly asked the farmer.

Her father answered, "He left several hours ago."

"What?" she cried. "He left without saying good-bye? After *all* we had together? I mean, *last night* he made such passionate *love* to me."

"What?" shouted the father. "He took *advantage* of you?"

The farmer ran out into the front yard looking for the man, but by now the man was halfway up the side of a mountain. The farmer screamed up at him, "I'm gonna get you! You had sex with my daughter!"

The man looked back down from the mountainside, cupped his hands next to his mouth, and yelled out, "I laid the old laDEE too!"

Q: What's the difference between karate and judo?
A: Karate is a martial art, and judo is what you use to make bagels.

A man and woman get married. On their wedding night, just as they're about to get into bed, the husband says to his bride, "There's something about me that I haven't told you, and I think that before we go any further in our marriage, you have a right to know."

The woman nervously asks, "What is it, dear?"

The man clears his throat and says, "Sweetheart, I just LOVE golf. I play it all day Saturday and Sunday, and at least two or three afternoons a week. The game gives me great joy, and even if I tried, I don't think I could ever change. Now that you know this about me, do you still want me for your husband?"

The woman takes her husband's hands into her own, looks into his eyes, and says with relief, "Darling, of course I still want to be with you. But now I have something I have to tell you." She takes a deep breath, then tells him, "Honey, up to now I've been a hooker."

"Is that all?" replies the husband. "Golly, all you have to do is aim a little bit more to the left. . . ."

Q: Why do WASPs love to play golf?
A: It's the only time they get to dress like pimps.

A man is out playing golf at his country club on a beautiful, sunny Saturday afternoon. He plays a few holes, and then he catches up to a group of people who are taking a long time on the green. The man waits and waits, but these people are moving so slowly that the man eventually gets very annoyed.

He is about to go up and say something to them, when he sees a country club official walking toward the group. The golfer goes over to the official and says, "Hey! What's with those people? I'm really getting aggravated! They're playing so slowly that—"

The country club official quickly interrupts him. "Shhh! Please keep your voice down so they don't hear you!" he says. "Those people are blind. We have a special program today so that they can come out here and find out what it's like to play a game of golf."

"Oh . . ." the golfer says. "Well, that's a really nice idea, but couldn't they play at *night*?"

A boy comes home from school and tells his father, "Dad! I had sex with my schoolteacher!"

The father smiles and says, "Well, you're a mite young, but the day a boy loses his virginity is a day to celebrate. And as congratulations, son, let's go downtown. I'll take you out to dinner, and then we'll go buy you a brand-new bicycle!"

The boy replies, "Dinner sounds great, Dad, but could we wait a little on the bike?" The boy starts to rub his backside. "My butt," he says, "is still a little sore."

Q: What's a woman who is a 10 in New York?
A: A 2 with a good apartment.

A man and woman are getting undressed on their wedding night, when the bride says to the groom, "Be gentle with me, honey. I'm a virgin."

The husband is totally shocked. "How could you be a virgin?" he asks. "You've been married three times already!"

"I know," replies the bride, "but my first husband was an artist, and all he wanted to do was *look* at my body. My second husband was a psychiatrist, and all he wanted to do was *talk* about it. And my third husband was a lawyer, and he just kept saying, 'I'll get back to you next week!'

▼▼▼

A guy goes into a clock store and goes up to the service department. He unzips his pants, takes out his penis, and puts it on the counter. The woman behind the counter says, "Sir, this is a *clock* store, not a *cock* store."

"I know," replies the man. "I'd like a face and two hands on this, please."

Q: How many Irishmen does it take to change a lightbulb?

A: Two. One to hold the lightbulb, and the other to drink until the room spins.

Miss Smith, a society matron in Mobile, Alabama, has a problem. Several of her young female charges do not have dates for the big debutante ball coming up. Miss Smith tells the girls not to worry, that she will think of something to do about this.

She finally decides to call the nearby military base. When she is put through to the commanding officer, in her most charming southern accent, she says, "Sir, my name is Miss Smith and I am having a debutante ball this Friday night. Unfortunately, a few of my girls don't have dates for the dance, and I was wondering: Would you be able to send a few of your finest young officers over on Friday evening at eight o'clock?"

The commanding officer says to the woman, "Why, yes, I think that some of our officers would love to attend your little soiree."

"Thank you so much," replies the woman. "And by the way, I do have two strict requirements."

"Yes?" asks the officer.

"Well, first," says Miss Smith, her accent making her sound like the southern belle that she is, "I want the men to be dressed in their finest dress whites, looking just as sharp as can be. My second condition is, of course, no Jews."

"It will be arranged," says the commander.

Friday night arrives, and the girls are all in the ballroom of the country mansion, dressed in their formal gowns. Several of the girls are without dates, standing alone. Precisely at the appointed hour, a jeep pulls up in front of the building. Six large black officers get out of the jeep, dressed in their finest formal white uniforms.

Miss Smith hurries over to them and says, "Can I help you men?"

One of the officers says, "Yes, ma'am. We're here to meet our dates."

"Why . . . why . . ." stammers Miss Smith, "there must be some mistake!"

"No, ma'am," says one of the officers. "*You* might make mistakes, and *I* might make mistakes, but Colonel Goldberg, he *never* makes mistakes."

■◄▼

Q: What do lite beer and making love in a rowboat have in common?

A: They're both fucking close to water.

▚▚▚

An Englishman got into my cab one night and told me to take him to a certain address on West Seventy-second Street. "That's just a few doors down from the Dakota," I said, "where your fellow Englishman, John Lennon, used to live."

"Yes, I know," replied the man. "My ex-wife was standing ten feet away from him when he was shot. My main regret is that the blighter had such bloody good aim."

"This was your ex-wife?" I asked.

"Yes," he said. "I'm in the middle of a lawsuit with her. She is still using my title, quite illegally, you understand. But with your ridiculous American divorce laws, she got an estate that had been in my family for three centuries, and so I had to buy it back from her. Even that I could tolerate, but I won't allow her to continue to use my title."

"What is your title?" I asked.

"I'm an English lord," he said. "You know, Americans are so impressed with titles. I don't mind, really, but I did get rather annoyed at a party once when this American woman kept calling me Mister Lord."

"A lord, eh?" I said. "Well, I must say, I'm impressed. I guess that means that I'm an American."

"Yes," said his lordship, "you probably are. You know, one day a friend of mine in the Houses of Par-

liament was walking up a staircase on the side of a great hall. My friend, a well-respected lord in Parliament, looked across the hall and saw the Lord of Limerick going down the staircase on the other side.

"The Lord of Limerick had just come from a photo session, and was wearing his ermines and all his jewels. My friend needed to talk to the Lord of Limerick about a debate that was soon going to be occurring in the Houses of Parliament. Since these two lords are of the same stature, my friend could address the Lord of Limerick by his first name.

"So he called across the hall to him, 'Neil!' The Lord of Limerick did not hear him, so my friend called out again, this time louder, 'NEIL!' At that moment, fifty American tourists got down on their knees. The next day, that story made the front page of the London Times!"

❖❖❖

Q: What can a swan do that a duck can't, and that a lawyer should?
A: Shove his bill up his ass.

❖❖❖

A guy is walking down Eleventh Avenue late one evening when a prostitute comes up to him and says lasciviously, "I'll do *anything* you want for a hundred dollars, if you can name it in three words."

"Anything?" asks the incredulous man. "Anything at all?"

The hooker winks at him, smiles, and says, "Anything!"

The man thinks for just a moment, then says, "Paint . . . my . . . house."

Q: What's the address of the gay page on the Internet?

A: C: Enter

Three hookers are sitting around discussing the pet names that they call their boyfriends. One of them says, "Well, I call my boyfriend Coca-Cola, because he's got the real thing, and I gets it whenever I wants it."

The second one chimes in, "Well, I call my boyfriend 7-Up, because he has seven inches and I gets it whenever I wants it."

They both turn to the third prostitute and ask, "So what do you call *your* man?"

The third prostitute smiles and replies, "I calls him Courvoisier."

"Courvoisier?" says the first hooker. "Ain't that some fancy liquor?"

The third hooker just grins, nods her head, and slowly says, "Uh-huh."

Q: What does a blonde say after multiple orgasms?
A: "You mean you *all* play for the same team?"

A Polish guy is walking down a dark street when he is suddenly attacked by four muggers. He fights likes hell, but eventually the muggers wrestle him to the ground. It takes all four of them to hold him down, but they manage to go through his pockets. However, the muggers are incredulous when all they find is forty-three cents. "You mean you fought that hard for a lousy forty-three cents?" asks one of the robbers.

"That's all you wanted?" groans the Pole. "I thought you were after the four hundred dollars in my shoe."

Two school administrators are talking about the drug problem in their public schools. One of the administrators says, "You know, we reduced the drug problem in our school just with the use of graphic art."

"Really!" exclaims the other man. "What did you do?"

The first man says, "Well, we made posters and got a hundred of them printed up. On the left side of the poster, we had a big circle. Underneath it, we wrote, 'This is your brain.' On the right side of the poster we had a little tiny circle and underneath it we wrote, 'This is your brain on drugs.' It's simple, it's direct, and it was very effective. By putting these posters up all over our school, we were able to reduce the drug problem by *forty percent!*"

The other administrator replies, "That's very interesting, because we did a similar thing in *our* school, but in *our* school we were able to reduce the drug problem by *ninety-five* percent."

"That's amazing!" says the first administrator. "What did you do?"

The second administrator explains, "Well, we *also* had posters made up. They were very similar to yours, but on *our* poster, we had a little tiny circle on the *left* side. Underneath it we put, 'This is your asshole.' On the *right* side of the poster we had a very large circle, and underneath that we put, 'This is your asshole in prison.'"

◆◆◆

Q: What is the difference between a G-spot and a golf ball?
A: A man will spend *hours* looking for a golf ball.

◆◆◆

A grandmother in Miami wants to take her grandson to the beach, but her daughter won't let her. The grandmother says, "I'll take good care of him, I'll watch him every minute, nothing bad will happen, I promise."

So the daughter finally relents. "Okay," she says. 'Good. Go."

So the grandmother takes her grandson to the

beach, and the little boy is running up and down the beach, throwing stones in the ocean and looking for shells. The grandmother is watching him carefully as the grandson crouches down to pick up a shell. All of a sudden a huge wave comes in, splashes over the boy, and sweeps him out to sea.

The grandmother starts to panic. "Oh my God!" she cries out. "Help! Help!" She looks around, but there is no one else on the beach. So she starts weeping, and begins to pray. "Dear Lord," she manages to say between her sobs, "please bring him back! I'll do anything! I'll go to the synagogue, I'll keep kosher, I'll give money to Israel. Anything you want, God! Please! Just bring him back."

All of a sudden, a wave washes in to the shore, depositing the child back on the beach, dry as a bone. The grandmother looks at the little boy and is overwhelmed with happiness. Suddenly, though, she becomes irritated. She looks up to the sky and calls out, "HE HAD A HAT!"

Q: How do you make holy water?
A: Put some water in a pan and boil the hell out of it.

A golfer is walking down the fairway, when he spots a buddy of his a couple of yards away. "Hey, Joe," he calls out, "how are ya doin'?"

Joe turns around and in an incredibly raspy voice replies, "Pretty good, Bob. How are you?"

"My God!" says Bob. "What happened to your voice?"

"Well, the other day I was out playing the back nine," says Joe, in a voice so scratchy sounding that it is almost painful for his friend to listen to, "and I sliced a ball way off into the rough. I got all pissed off and threw my club down. I ran over and was rooting through the weeds, looking around the trees, but I couldn't find my ball *anywhere*."

Joe continues in his whispery voice, "A couple of yards away there is this foursome of women playing, and I'm looking all over and I can't find the ball. Just off the rough there is this cow grazing, so I'm wandering around, looking everywhere, and I walk over near the cow."

Joe's voice seems to be getting weaker, but he wheezes on, "I lift up his tail, and sticking there in the cow's ass is a golf ball. So I check it out and it doesn't have my mark on it. So I yell out to the women, 'Hey! Does this look like yours?'" Joe motions toward his throat and rasps, "She hit me in the neck with a nine-iron."

■▼■

Q: Did you hear about the new NFL franchise that will have an all-gay roster?

A: They plan to be a real come-from-behind team.

▼▼▼

Late one night, two hookers are standing on their usual corner when one of them says to the other, "How has your night been so far?"

"Kind of interesting," replies the second prostitute.

"Really?" says the first. "What happened?"

"Well," begins the woman, "earlier tonight, a man came up to me here on the corner and asked if we could go back into the alley. I said, 'Sure.'

"When we got to that dark place behind the liquor store, the man asked me, 'How much would it cost to have sex with you?'

"I told him, 'A hundred bucks.'

"'Gee, I don't have that much,' he said. So I told him, 'Well, I could give you a blow job for fifty.'

"He said, 'Golly, I don't have that much either.' By that point, I was starting to get a little annoyed.

"'Just how much *do* you have?' I asked. He dug deep down into his pocket, fished around, then pulled out this crumpled-up twenty-dollar bill.

"I said, 'Twenty dollars? That's it? Well, I suppose I could give you a hand job for twenty bucks.'

"'Gosh,' he said, 'I don't know.'

"He just stood there thinking about it until I said, 'Well . . . ?'

"Finally, he made up his mind. 'Gee . . . uh . . . okay,' he said. So he unzipped his pants and, much to my surprise, he pulled out the biggest dick that I've ever seen in my life!"

"Wow!" says the first hooker. "What did you do?"

"What *could* I do?" replies the second hooker. "I loaned him eighty bucks."

* * *

A flasher was thinking of retiring, but he decided to stick it out for another year.

* * *

A grizzled-looking cowboy bursts into a saloon, goes over to the bar, and pounds loudly with his fist. The bartender rushes over and the cowboy snarls, "I just got off the range! I'm hot, I'm dusty, and I'm so thirsty that I could lick the sweat off a bull's balls!"

Over in the corner, a slightly built cowboy dressed in pink chimes sweetly, "Moooo, moooooo . . ."

* * *

Two employees are talking. One of them asks the other, "How long have you been working here?"

The other one replies, "Since they threatened to fire me."

* * *

Three mice are standing around talking. These are three very macho mice, and they are all trying to outdo each other. The first mouse says, "You know those little pellets they put out around the house trying to poison us? I *love* those things. I eat them like candy."

The second mouse is not to be outdone. "Oh yeah?" he says. "Well, you know those mousetraps they put out to try and catch us? What I do is get on the trap, grab the cheese, and then flip over onto my back, and when the bar comes swinging down I grab it and do bench presses with it."

The third mouse says to the other two, "You guys are two tough mice, and I'd love to keep hanging out with you here, but I've got to go fuck the cat."

Q: What's the definition of a gentleman?
A: Someone who can play the accordion and *won't*.

A Polish man, his wife, and a single man are shipwrecked on a deserted island. They decide that one of them should climb up high into a palm tree and be the lookout for any passing ships. The single man quickly volunteers to take the first watch. He climbs up the tree, and after a few minutes he shouts down to the couple, "HEY! QUIT FUCKING DOWN THERE! STOP THAT FUCKING!"

The Polish man and woman look at each other quizzically. Not only are they not fooling around at all, but they are standing ten feet apart. "Man, what a NUT!" says the husband to the wife.

The man in the tree is quiet for a few minutes, but then begins shouting again, "BREAK IT UP, I SAID! STOP THAT FUCKING!" This goes on for several hours. Finally the husband says to his wife, "Maybe I'd better go up there and relieve him for a while."

As soon as the husband is high up in the tree, the single man jumps on the wife and proceeds to screw her like crazy. The Polish man looks down and sees them. "You know," he says to himself, "from up here it really *does* look like they're fucking down there!"

Q: What do being in the Mafia and eating pussy have
   in common?
A: One slip of the tongue and you're in deep shit.

A sailor arrives at port after having been at sea for
six months. Being extremely horny, the first thing he
does upon setting foot on terra firma is to head
straight to the nearest brothel.

He goes right up to the madam and says, "How
much?"

The madam replies that her girls charge two hundred dollars and that she has only one immediately
available. The sailor feels that this seems a bit pricey,
but in his desperate condition he has no choice. He
agrees to the terms and is shown upstairs to a room
to await the arrival of the woman.

When the hooker gets to the room, she opens the
door only to find the sailor furiously jerking off. "Wait
a minute!" cries the hooker. "What are you doing?"

The sailor looks up at her and answers, "Hey, for
two hundred bucks you don't think I'm going to let
you have the easy one, do you?"

*I was talking one evening to a businessman. He told
me that he had been waiting in line at the bank that*

day, when suddenly thieves burst in and began a robbery. "The most remarkable thing about the whole incident," the man said, "was that during the entire time that the bank was being held up, no one *got out of line!*"

▼▼▼

One day, the President of the United States receives a call on his red telephone in the Oval Office. When he picks up the receiver, he hears a friendly voice on the line. It is the president of Russia. "Hello!" greets the American president. "How are you?"

"I'm fine," answers the Russian president, "but I need to ask a favor of you."

The American says, "I'll be happy to help if I can. What is it?"

"You know," the Russian confides, "this whole AIDS thing has gotten us pretty worried over here. We've run out of condoms. We need ten million more condoms right away, but our manufacturers just can't handle that kind of volume. Do you think that you could rush me a shipment of seven million condoms next week?"

"I'll make some calls and see what I can do," replies the President.

"Just one more favor," says the Russian. "We need all the condoms to be sixteen inches long."

"I'll do my best and get back to you right away," says the President.

They hang up and the President immediately telephones the largest condom manufacturer in the United States. When he gets the head of the company on the phone, he says, "Hello, this is the President."

The manufacturer is astonished. "Mr. President! What an honor to have you call! Is there anything that I can do for you?"

"Well, actually there is," says the President. "I need to ask you for a favor."

"Anything!" exclaims the manufacturer.

"I just got a call from the president of Russia," the President explains. "The AIDS situation has gotten them pretty scared over there, and they need some more condoms. Could you ship out an order of seven million condoms to them as early as next week?"

"Of course, Mr. President," says the manufacturer. "It will require some rescheduling, and our factories will have to run twenty-four hours a day, but I think that we can handle it."

"Thank you, sir," replies the President. "However, I do have another favor to ask of you."

"No problem," says the manufacturer. "What is it?"

"I would like," says the President, "for you to make all the condoms sixteen inches long. Could you do that?"

The manufacturer thinks for a moment, then replies, "Well, it will involve retooling some of our machines, but for you, Mr. President, I am very happy to do anything that I can."

"There's just one more favor I'd like to ask of you," says the President. "On these seven million sixteen-inch condoms, I would like for you to stamp 'Made in U.S.A.—MEDIUM.'"

Q: How many Zen Buddhists does it take to change a lightbulb?
A: Two. One to change the bulb, and the other not to change the bulb.

Back in the early 1960s, a television actor went to one of the major networks to audition for a new situation comedy. When he read his lines for the producers, everyone loved his performance. A few days later, the network executives called him in for a meeting.

"We loved your audition," said one of the executives to the actor. "We think you're very funny, and you have a great talent for physical humor. You're just what we're looking for. We have one problem, though. We don't think that your name will work. The country is just not ready for a television star named Penis Van Lesbian."

"But," protested the actor, "I think that Penis Van Lesbian is a great name! It's *very* catchy."

A long discussion followed, during which the network executives and the actor debated the merits of the name Penis Van Lesbian. Finally, the network promised to name the entire show after him, if the actor would only change his name.

The actor agreed, and the program went on to become a huge success. It was called *The Dick Van Dyke Show*.

■▼■

A woman told me that her mother called her from Florida and told her this joke:

Q: What's the most popular bra size in St. Petersburg?
A: Thirty-eight long.

■▼■

An Englishman is visiting New York. He loves jokes and is very anxious to take a typical American joke back with him to England. Every time he gets to a party or a gathering of any sort, he tries to get someone to tell him a typical American joke, but no one is forthcoming. He is in this country for two full weeks and has no luck hearing any American jokes. Finally, he is in the cab on his way out to Kennedy Airport, and he confides his predicament to the cab-driver.

"I'm on my way back to London," he explains, "and I'm very disappointed. I just love jokes, and during my entire stay here in this country I've been trying to hear a good, typical Yankee joke, but no one has been able to tell me a single one."

"Yeah?" says the cabdriver. "Well I got a joke I can tell ya."

"Oh! Yes! Yes!" exclaims the Englishman. "Do that, please!"

The cabbie says, "Okay. So dis chick is walkin' down da road, and she comes to a crossroads in da road. She looks to da right and comin' at her is dis guy joggin'. She looks forward and sees dis guy comin' on a bicycle. She looks to da left, and comin' at her is a guy on a horse. Which one knew her?"

The Englishman thinks for a moment, then replies, "I don't know."

"Da horse manure!" says the cabbie, and the Englishman bursts into laughter.

"By Jove!" he cries out between guffaws, "that is smashing! That is the funniest thing I've ever heard! I must tell everyone in London!"

So the Englishman boards his plane and chuckles to himself throughout the entire flight. The airliner lands at Heathrow and the man's wife meets him at the airport. He immediately tells her his new joke, but she doesn't laugh. The next day at work he tells all his colleagues the joke, and when he hits the punch line he laughs hysterically. Unfortunately, though, he is the only one laughing. That night, he goes to his club and tells the joke to his friends and peers, but it doesn't elicit any laughter. So now he is totally flummoxed.

Walking down the street a couple of days later, he runs into a friend in front of the Royal Albert Hall. "Oh, hello," says the friend. "How are you doing, old chap?"

"Lovely," says the guy. "Actually, I just got back from the States, and I heard this amazing joke. But no one I've told it to here laughs at it."

The friend suggests, "Well, why don't you try it out on me. I have a rather good sense of humor, if I do say so myself."

"Hmm," says the first guy, "yes, you do. All right, here it is: Apparently a young lady is strolling down the road and she comes upon a crossroads. To her right is a cyclist, directly ahead is a pedestrian, and to her left is an equestrian. Which one knew her?"

"I haven't the foggiest," answers the friend.

"Horseshit!" says the first guy. "And I think that's *damn* funny!"

◼◼◼

Q: How can you tell when your house has been burglarized by gays?
A: When you come home, you discover that your jewelry is missing, and all your furniture has been tastefully rearranged.

◼◼◼

A man is walking down the street, when a bum comes up to him and asks for a dollar. Being in a generous mood, the man pulls out a ten-dollar bill.

As he hands it to the bum, he says, "You're not going to use this for booze, are you?"

"I never drink," replies the bum solemnly.

"I hope you're not going to use it for gambling," says the man.

"I never gamble," the bum replies in earnest.

"Say," says the man, "would you mind coming home with me? I would really like for my wife to meet you."

"Me?" says the surprised bum. "Why me?"

"Well," the man explains, "I would like to show my wife what happens to a man who never drinks or gambles."

◆◆◆

A guy goes to the doctor, and the doctor says, "I'm going to need a urine sample, a semen sample, a blood sample, and a stool sample."

The guy says, "Listen, Doc, I'm in a hurry. Can I just leave my shorts?"

◆◆◆

Two little boys are sitting on the front steps of a brothel. All day long, they see men come up to the front of the building, take out their wallets, remove a hundred dollars, and go inside. A little while later, they see the men coming out, tucking in their shirts. By late afternoon, the boys are getting really curious as to what is happening in there.

They decide to pool their money and see how much they've got. After emptying their pockets and putting all their change in one pile, they count it up and they have seventy-eight cents between them. Then they walk up the steps and into the house of ill repute.

The madam greets them at the door. "Well, young men," she says, "what can I do for you?" One of the boys holds out his hand with all the change in it. The madam looks at the change for a moment, then says, "Seventy-eight cents, eh? Hmmm. Well, I think I can give you something for that. Come on upstairs."

The boys follow her up the steps and then into a room in which there is a naked woman. "Honey," the madam instructs the hooker, "lie down on the bed and spread your legs." The hooker does it, and then the madam says to one of the boys, "Come over here." She points to the spot between the hooker's legs and says, "Stick your nose in that."

The boy does it, and after about thirty seconds the madam says, "All right, stop. That's enough. Now go back and stand over there next to your friend." Then she motions to the other boy.

"Okay," she says, "now it's your turn. Go over and do the same thing." The second boy sticks his nose between the hooker's legs, and after thirty more seconds the madam says, "Stop. Now go and stand back over there next to your friend." When the boy does it, the madam says, "Well, fellas. That's it. That's seventy-eight cents' worth."

The little boys go back out onto the front steps and sit down, deep in thought. After about five minutes of sitting there in silence, one of the boys turns to the other and says, "You know . . . I don't think that I could *take* a hundred dollars' worth of that."

Q: What do you call a gay gentleman from the Deep South?
A: A homo-sex-you-all.

It was about four o'clock in the morning and I was nearing the end of my shift. My last fare had gotten out in Queens and I was driving back to Manhattan, when I saw a traffic light that must have been broken, because it went straight from green to red. I slammed on the brakes and managed to stop before I entered the intersection, but as I screeched to a halt, I heard something thump behind me. It sounded like something had fallen off the backseat.

It sounded too heavy to be an umbrella, and besides, it wasn't even raining, so I stretched around and looked down There, on of the floor of the cab, was an old brass lamp. I picked it up and as I looked at it, I noticed that it had gotten some dirt from the floor smudged on its side. So with the sleeve of my jacket I tried rubbing the dirt off.

No sooner had I done that than smoke started pouring out of the lamp, and before I knew it, there was a genie sitting on the front seat right beside me. Before I could gather my wits about me, the genie said, "I am a genie, and I am empowered to grant you one wish."

I just sat there stammering, until the impact of what he said struck me like a bolt of lightning. I knew immediately what I wanted. Without hesitation, I reached over into the glove compartment and pulled out a map of the world. I opened it up and said to the genie, "Do you see this? This is the earth. My wish is that there will be peace all over the world for the next million years. No wars, no fighting, and everyone living together in kindness, generosity, and brotherhood."

"Wow!" said the genie. "That's quite a tall order. Come on, now. I'm just a genie. I mean, that's a really tough request! Isn't there something *else* you want? Some task that might be *slightly* less daunting?"

I thought for a few moments, and then said, "Okay. How about this? I wish for you to make me the best drummer on the planet."

The genie thought for a moment, and then said, "Ummm . . . Let me take another look at that *map*."

■▼■

Did you hear about the Polish Godfather? He made someone an offer they couldn't understand.

🚕

A French couple, an Italian couple, and a Polish couple are enjoying a dinner party together. The Frenchman leans over to his lovely wife and says, "Please pass the sugar, sugar."

The Italian, not wanting to seem any less romantic than the Frenchman, puts his arm around his wife and says, "Please pass me the honey, honey."

Hearing this, the Polish man jumps to his feet and loudly says to his wife, "Pass me the pork, pig!"

🚕

Q: What do you call the stork who brings Polish babies?
A: A dope peddler.

🚕

Frank Sinatra hears that the Pope is going to be in town, so he goes out and gets a thousand-dollar suit. He then goes to the hall where the Pope is going to appear and sits down in the audience right in the front row. He happens to look over to his left and he sees, sitting in the seat right next to him, a bum with a urine-stained, decrepit suit, and a beat-up old hat. Sinatra is disgusted, can hardly stand the stink, and is about to change his seat, when from behind the curtain the Pope walks out. The Pope bows and then walks straight over to the bum. He leans down, whispers something into the bum's ear, and then walks back behind the curtain.

Sinatra is amazed at the Pope's compassion for the downtrodden. Hoping for a personal blessing for himself, Sinatra turns to the bum and says, "I'll make you a deal. I'll trade you this thousand-dollar suit for your clothes and hat, and I'll give you a hundred bucks besides. What do you say?"

The bum looks over with crossed, bloodshot eyes, and slurs, "Shertainly."

They walk out of the hall, trade clothes, and Sinatra goes back to his seat. A couple of minutes later, the Pope comes out from behind the curtain, looks directly at Sinatra, and immediately walks right over to him. He leans down and whispers in Sinatra's ear, "I thought I told you to get the fuck *outta* here."

Q: What's the similarity between a lawyer and a trombone player?

A: Everybody is really relieved when they finally close the case.

A teacher is instructing her third-grade pupils about three-syllable words. She asks them to think of a word with three syllables and use it in a sentence. Dirty Ernie raises his hand and waves it frantically. The teacher calls instead on Jennifer.

"Beautiful," says Jennifer sweetly. "My teacher is beautiful."

"That's very nice," says the teacher. "Anyone else?"

Ernie starts waving his arms, but the teacher chooses Freddy instead.

"Wonderful," replies Freddy. "My teacher is wonderful."

"You're so kind," says the teacher. "Now, does anyone have another word?" Ernie almost becomes hysterical, waving his arm and almost jumping out of his seat. "All right, Ernie," she says. "Go ahead."

"Urinate," says Ernie.

The teacher is shocked. "Ernie!" she cries.

"Urinate, but if your legs were better, you'd be a ten!"

■▼■

A doctor says to his elderly patient, "I've got some bad news for you. You have AIDS and Alzheimer's disease."

"Oh, whew," gasps the old man. "Thank God I don't have AIDS!"

■▼■

The first manned space voyage goes to Mars. When the astronauts finally touch down on the surface of the red planet, they look around at the unusual landscape. They climb down the ladder, and as soon as they set foot on the strange planet, they see an odd-looking vehicle driving right toward them. It quickly pulls up to within ten feet of where the astronauts are standing, then stops.

The door opens and a Martian gets out. "Where are you from?" asks the Martian in perfect English.

One of the astronauts draws himself up to his full height and proudly announces, "We're from Earth!"

"Oh, wow!" exclaims the Martian. "You're from Earth! Do you know a guy named . . ."

■▗▖■

Q: What's the ultimate in rejection?
A: When you're masturbating and your hand falls asleep.

■▗▖■

A man is sitting on a park bench when a friend of his comes walking by. "Hey, Frank!" says the walking man. "How are ya doin'?"

"Oh, I'm doing great," says the man on the bench, holding up a book. "I just finished reading this fantastic book on logic."

"Logic?" says the friend. "What do you mean?"

"Well, it teaches you to use your deductive reasoning powers."

The guy scratches his head and says, "I still don't quite follow you."

"Okay," says Frank, "I'll give you an example. Do you have an aquarium?"

"Well, yeah, I do," replies the guy.

"Now, you see," Frank begins to explain, "from that I would deduce that you probably like fish."

The guy says, "Yeah, that's true."

Then Frank continues, "So taking that one step farther, I would assume that you like water and that you probably like the ocean."

"Right," says the guy, becoming more and more interested.

Frank goes on, "And now I would say that you probably enjoy lying on the beach next to the ocean."

"Right again," replies the friend, now totally fascinated.

"So now I think that you would enjoy seeing a beautiful woman walking down the beach in a bikini."

"Yeah . . . ," concedes the man.

"And from that," Frank concludes, "I would deduce that you are a heterosexual."

"Yeah, that's true," says the man.

"Now, you see," Frank says triumphantly, "I got all that information just by asking you *one* question and then using logic."

"Wow, that is great!" says the friend, obviously impressed. "Could I possibly borrow that book from you?"

Frank hands the book to his pal and says, "Here. I just finished it. Take it home and enjoy it."

So the guy goes home that night and reads a little bit of the book. The next day he is walking down the street when he sees another one of his friends.

"Hey Lou," he says, "I gotta tell ya about this great book I've been reading on logic."

"Logic?" says Lou. "What do you mean?"

"I'll give you an example," says the man. "Do you have an aquarium?"

Lou replies, "No, I don't."

The guy exclaims, "You're a fucking faggot!"

◆◆◆

Q: Why can't witches have children?
A: Because their husbands have hollow wienies.

◆◆◆

A man told me that he came home late one evening and was standing talking with his doorman for a few minutes. The doorman said, "You won't believe what happened tonight."

"What?" said the man.

"This hooker walked by," said the doorman, "and she looked in, so I started talking to her. After a little while I said to her, 'How much for a hand job?'

"The hooker said, 'Fifteen bucks. You want one?'

"So I said, 'Nah, I just wanted to know how much I'd be saving if I did it myself.'"

◆◆◆

Two archaeologists are digging deep inside one of the Egyptian pyramids, when they suddenly break through a wall and find themselves inside a spectacular ancient tomb. They both gasp, and then they slowly begin to make their way around a room filled with ancient Egyptian artifacts. The archaeologists are awestruck at the richness of their find. They discover hieroglyphics, statues, many gold works of art, and chests full of jewels beyond what they could have ever imagined in their wildest dreams.

Suddenly one of them shouts, "Look!"

Lo and behold, over in a dusty corner, lies a mummy. They walk over to get a better look, and are amazed at how well it seems to be preserved. They are transfixed as they stare in amazement at how skillfully the mummy has been wrapped in its bandages.

Suddenly, one of the men exclaims, "I have an idea! We have a heart-resuscitation unit with us! Why don't we hook it up to the mummy and see what happens?"

The other guy says, "Great idea! What have we got to lose?"

So they get the heart-resuscitation unit and carefully hook all the wires up to the long-dead pharaoh. When they are all set to go, one of the men turns the knob up to 3 and the other man pushes the red activation button. The unit starts humming, and the mummy starts vibrating, but as soon as the man takes his finger off the red button, all motion stops.

The other man says, "Let's try it again," and he turns the knob up to 6. The button man puts his finger on the red button and presses. Once again, the mummy starts to vibrate, but as soon as the man takes his finger off the button, all is quiet and still inside the tomb.

Without saying a word to each other, they both decide to go for broke. One man cranks the knob all the way up to 11 and the other man hits the button and just lays on it for the longest time. The mummy starts vibrating, and then begins to shake and twitch. The man yanks his finger off of the button, but the mummy continues to shake more and more violently.

Suddenly, the torso begins to rise slowly up off the table.

"Oh my God," cries one of the archaeologists, "it's alive! It's starting to sit up!"

When the mummy reaches a sitting position, it

slowly opens its mouth and lets out a little cough. A small cloud of dust puffs through the mummified lips.

"It's gonna say something! Oh my God! It's gonna talk!"

In a voice that sounds like it's coming through a throat that has been parched for centuries, the mummy rasps, *"Is Dick Clark still alive?"*

🔲🔲🔲

Q: What do you get when you cross a black guy and a fish?
A: Fillet of soul brother.

🔲🔲🔲

A farmer gets sent to jail, and his wife is trying to hold the farm together until her husband can get out. She's not, however, very good at farm work, so she writes a letter to him in jail: "Dear Sweetheart, I want to plant the potatoes. When is the best time to do it?"

The farmer writes back: "Honey, don't go near that field. That's where all my guns are buried."

But, because he is in jail all of the farmer's mail is censored. So when the sheriff and his deputies read this, they all run out to the farm and dig up the entire potato field looking for guns. After two full days of digging, they don't find one single weapon.

The farmer then writes to his wife: "Honey, *now* is when you should plant the potatoes."

🔲🔲🔲

Q: What's the difference between a wife and a mistress?
A: About twenty-five pounds.

Q: What's the difference between a husband and a boyfriend?
A: About forty-five minutes.

An Italian guy and a Jewish guy go out to dinner. They go to a very expensive restaurant and are there for a couple of hours, talking and carrying on. Finally the waiter comes over and says, "Who should I give the check to?"

The Italian guy says, "Give it to me. I'll take care of everything."

"Fine," says the waiter.

The next day the headlines read, "Jewish Ventriloquist Strangled to Death."

Q: What's the difference between a gay and a straight rodeo?
A: In a straight rodeo, they all say, "*Ride* them suckers!"

Two Irish women are working in the garden together, and one of them, Molly, pulls a carrot out of the ground. "Oh, my, Kathleen," she says, "this carrot really reminds me of Seamus."

"Oh, does it, now?" asks Kathleen with a slight chuckle. "And what is it about this carrot that reminds you of Seamus? Is it the *length*, maybe?"

"No, no," says Molly, "it's not the length of it that reminds me of Seamus."

"Well, then," Kathleen inquires, flushing a bit, "is it maybe the *breadth* that reminds you of Seamus?"

"No," answers Molly, "it's not the breadth that reminds me of him, either."

"Good Lord," asks Kathleen, "then what exactly is it about that carrot that reminds you so much of Seamus?"

"Well," replies Molly, "it's the *dirt* all over it."

■▾■

A man goes to the doctor. "Doc," he says, "every time I sneeze I get an orgasm!"

"My goodness," replies the doctor. "What are you taking for it?"

The man says, "Pepper."

■▾■

Every autumn, a little-known football rivalry between two colleges in Boston is played out on the gridiron of a small university in the Polish section of town, Kowalski U. For the last five years, Kowalski U. has crushed their archrivals, the world-famous Massachusetts Institute of Technology.

Although MIT is large in stature within the academic world and small in stature on the football field, just the opposite is true, of course, for Kowalski U. Therefore, each year the hulking players of Kowalski U. have mercilessly taunted and humiliated the defeated coaches and players of MIT after winning the big game.

This year, however, the MIT coach has devised a plan that he hopes will ensure his team's victory. Suspecting that Kowalski's star quarterback cannot meet the minimum academic requirements for athletes, the coach arranges to have the Commissioner of Education on the field just before kickoff to give him a surprise test.

Saturday arrives and the stadium is packed with home-team Kowalski fans. Both teams take the field for the opening kickoff, and the cheerleaders are leading the crowd in a rousing victory chant.

Suddenly, everything comes to a halt when the announcer states over the public address system that Kowalski's star quarterback must take a test right then and there on the field to prove that he is eligible to play. Both teams crowd around the Commissioner and the quarterback at the center of the field as the test begins. "There will be three questions," he says, "and you must answer them all correctly in order to play this game today."

The quarterback nervously wipes his brow as the cheerleaders get the crowd shouting in unison, "PASS THE TEST! PASS THE TEST! PASS THE TEST!"

"First question," says the Commissioner as the

crowd hushes. "Who was the first President of the United States?"

The quarterback swallows hard, thinks for several moments, then answers, "George Washington?"

"That is correct!" states the Commissioner, and the crowd begins to chant, "ONE DOWN, TWO TO GO! ONE DOWN, TWO TO GO!"

"Next question," says the Commissioner. "Spell the word 'dog'."

The quarterback digs his toe into the ground and begins to fidget. A full minute goes by and then he finally says, "D-O-G?"

The crowd lets out a roar and then begins to chant, "TWO DOWN, ONE TO GO! TWO DOWN, ONE TO GO!"

The Commissioner says, "This is your final question. If you answer this correctly, you will be able to lead your team on the field today." The crowd falls silent, and the tension becomes so thick that one of the fans tries to cut it with a kielbasa knife.

"Okay," says the Commissioner, "here we go: What is ten plus five?"

Immediately, the quarterback begins to pace back and forth. Suddenly he stops and looks up at the sky. The sweat begins to pour off of him as he puts his hand on his forehead, closes his eyes, and mutters to himself, "Ten plus five . . . Ten plus five . . . Ten plus five . . ." He turns to the Commissioner, looks him straight in the eye, and says, "Fifteen?"

The crowd chants loudly, "GIVE HIM ANOTHER CHANCE! GIVE HIM ANOTHER CHANCE!"

Q: Why is a bachelor skinny and a married man fat?
A: The bachelor comes home, takes one look at what's in the refrigerator, and goes to bed. The married man comes home, takes one look at what's in the bed, and goes to the refrigerator.

On one of my days off, I was taking a taxi myself, and talking to the cabdriver. When I told him that I was also a driver, he said to me, "I just love this job, and I love it for three reasons: Number one, every day is payday. Each night when I get home I have that cash in my pocket.

"Number two, I'm my own boss. I can take a break anytime and I've got nobody looking over my shoulder.

"Number three, I work when I want to. I used to get fired for that!"

A guy walks out of a house of ill repute and sits down on a park bench, deep in thought. "Man!" he says to himself. "What a business! You've got it. You sell it. And you've *still got it!*"

Q: What's the difference between heaven and hell?
A: *In heaven:*
   the policemen are English
   the cooks are French
   the mechanics are German
   the lovers are Italian
   and the whole thing is run by the Swiss

   In hell:
   the policemen are German
   the cooks are English
   the mechanics are French
   the lovers are Swiss
   and the whole thing is run by the Italians

▼▼▼ ■

Three Frenchmen and an American woman are having dinner together. At one point during the conversation, the term 'savoir faire' is used by one of the Frenchmen. The American woman says, "Excuse me, gentlemen, but I don't know what that means. What is the definition of 'savoir faire'?"

"Ah," says one of the Frenchmen, "it does not translate directly into English, but I think I can give you a *feeling* for what 'savoir faire' means.

"As an example," he continues, "suppose that a man comes home unexpectedly from a long business trip. He goes upstairs to the bedroom, opens the door, and finds his wife in bed with another man. He says, 'Oh, excuse me.' *That*, my friend, is *savoir faire*."

The second Frenchman cuts in, "Pardon me, please, but that is not really the *true* meaning of savoir faire. It is very cool, I admit, but it is not savoir faire. *Real* savoir faire is when a man comes home from a long business trip, goes upstairs to the bedroom, opens the door, and finds his wife in bed with another man. The husband says, 'Oh, excuse me. *Please continue*.' Now, *that* is savoir faire."

The third Frenchman says, "Ah, I must admit, that is very close to an accurate definition of savoir faire, but it is not quite right. Real, true savoir faire is when a man comes home unexpectedly from a long business trip, goes upstairs to the bedroom, opens the door, and finds his wife in bed with another man. The husband says, 'Oh, excuse me. Please continue.' If the man continues, *that* is savoir faire."

■▀▄

Q: What's the difference between a woman with PMS and a terrorist?
A: You can negotiate with a terrorist.

■▀▄

A Polish airliner comes in for a landing at La Guardia Airport. As it approaches the runway, the pilot gets really scared that he's not going to make it, so he quickly reverses the thrust on the jet engines, and as soon as the wheels touch the landing strip he jams on the brakes. The plane comes to a screeching halt.

"Whew!" he gasps to the copilot, who is picking up his hat. "That was so close, I wasn't sure if we were going to make it! That has got to be the shortest runway I've ever seen in my life!"

"Yeah!" exclaims the copilot. "And did you also notice how *wide* it is?"

■▀▄

Q: What's black and brown and looks good on a lawyer?
A: A Doberman.

■▀▄

A man gave me this list, which he said came off the Internet:

Bumper Stickers

1. I love animals, they taste great.
2. EARTH FIRST! We'll strip-mine the other planets later.
3. "Very funny, Scotty. Now beam down my clothes."
4. Friends help you move. Real friends help you move bodies.
5. "Criminal Lawyer" is a redundancy.
6. Make it idiot proof and someone will make a better idiot.
7. He who laughs last thinks slowest.
8. Give me ambiguity or give me something else.
9. A flashlight is a case for holding dead batteries.
10. All generalizations are false, including this one.
11. Hard work has a future payoff. Laziness pays off now.
12. I won't rise to the occasion, but I'll slide over to it.
13. Consciousness: that annoying time between naps.
14. I don't suffer from insanity. I enjoy every minute of it.
15. Where there's a will, I want to be in it.
16. Okay, who put the "stop payment" on my reality check?
17. Few women admit their age. Few men act theirs.

18. We have enough youth. How about a fountain of SMART?

Q: How does a Jewish-American Princess change a lightbulb?
A: She says, "Daddy, I want a new apartment."

A very rich old man decides that when he dies he wants to take it with him. So he calls in a priest, a minister, and a rabbi and tells them, "You're the only people I can trust. I'm going to give you each a box containing a million dollars. At my funeral I want you to come up and put the three boxes into my coffin."

A couple of months later the old man dies and they have a big funeral with his body lying in state. Before the memorial service begins, the priest walks up to the casket and drops his box in. Then the minister goes up and puts his box next to the body. Finally, the rabbi goes up and places his box inside the coffin.

After the funeral, the three clergymen are together, riding away from the cemetery in a limousine. Suddenly the priest breaks out in a sweat and he starts getting all fidgety. The other two men look at him and the rabbi asks, "What's the matter with you?"

The priest says, nervously, "I just can't take this. I have to confess. I took seven hundred fifty thousand of that money and spent it on the new church we were building and the new school we needed. I just felt it was more important to do God's work here on earth, and so I took it. But now I feel terrible about it."

"Oh, whew," gasps the minister, looking extremely relieved. "I'm really glad that you admitted that. Because, you see, I myself took out nine hundred thousand dollars and put it toward that new food program for the homeless that we just started. I felt just exactly the same way you did, that it was more important to do God's work here in the world."

At this point the rabbi looks aghast at the two other men. "I'm shocked," he exclaims, "*shocked!* Why, I put my own personal check for the *entire amount* in that coffin!"

A Chinese man and his wife start to make love. They start to get into it, and when it starts getting really hot, the man says to the woman, "How about a little sixty-nine?"

The woman jumps out of the bed and says angrily, "How can you think of chicken broccoli at a time like this?"

A man dies and goes to heaven. As Saint Peter is welcoming him at the Pearly Gates, the man confesses to the saint, "To be quite honest, sir," he says, "I'm really surprised to be here."

"Why is that?" asks Saint Peter.

"Well, to tell you the truth," says the man, "I never believed in this place. I never thought that heaven really existed."

"*That* doesn't matter, my friend," replies the saint. "You see, up here we go by *results*. You were a good man, you were very generous, and you helped a lot of people. That's really all that matters. We don't care what you believed, as long as you led a decent, moral life."

Saint Peter continues, "However, I *do* have one problem. I'm just not quite sure where to put you."

"What do you mean?" asks the man.

"Do you see that big golden mosque over there?" Saint Peter asks, pointing to a cloud bank over to his right. "That's for the Moslems. That big marble temple in the cloud bank behind you is for the Jews, and that big wood-carved church over there is for the Presbyterians."

Saint Peter begins pointing all around. "The Hindus are over there, Episcopalians over there, the Rastafarians actually *created* those clouds over there to the left—"

"Saint Peter," the man interrupts, "what's that big, tall, black building in that cloud bank over there behind you?"

"Oh," says Saint Peter, "that's for the *Catholics*."

"But why doesn't it have any doors or windows?" asks the man.

"Well," says Saint Peter, lowering his voice, "that's because *they* think they're the only ones up here."

Q: What do you call a combination aphrodisiac and laxative?
A: Easy Come, Easy Go.

A scientist is conducting a survey on international sexual practices. He gets subjects from all over the world and asks them the same question: What do you do at the end of the sex act that makes your wife go crazy?

The first subject, a Japanese man, responds with, "I take rose petals and sprinkle them all over her naked body. Then I gently blow them off. It drives her crazy!"

The second subject, a Frenchman, reveals, "I take very expensive champagne and splash it all over her naked body. Then I lick it off. This drives her crazy!"

The third subject, an Italian guy from New York, says, "After I fuck my wife, I wipe my dick on the curtains. It drives her fucking crazy."

An out-of-towner driving east on Forty-sixth Street at Madison Avenue pulls his car up next to a New Yorker and asks, "How far is it to Fifth Avenue?"

The New Yorker considers it for a moment, then tells the man, "The way you're going, about twenty-four thousand miles."

A black man dies and goes to heaven. When he reaches the Pearly Gates he is met by Saint Peter.

"Welcome," says the saint. "You are about to enter the kingdom of heaven. Before I can let you in, however, I must ask you one question. What is the most magnificently stupendous thing that you ever did?"

"Oh, that's easy," replies the black man. "During the Mississippi–Alabama football game, underneath the grandstand, I boffed the granddaughter of the Grand Dragon of the KKK."

"Wow! That really *is* amazing!" exclaims Saint Peter. "Exactly when did you do that?"

The black man replies, "About five minutes ago."

Q: Why do Texans wear ten-gallon hats?
A: You can't cram all that shit into a derby.

A nightclub has a sign in the window: "Party Tonight! Come dressed as a mood!"

As evening approaches, a man shows up dressed completely in red. The man at the door looks at him and asks, "What emotion are you?"

The man replies, "I'm red with rage."

So he is let into the club. A few minutes later a woman comes up wearing green from head to toe. "I'm green with envy," she declares, and she is also welcomed into the club.

The next person to arrive is a man who is completely naked with his dick in a jar of pudding. The man at the door asks, "What the hell are you supposed to be?"

The naked man says, "I'm fucking disgusted!"

Or the variation with the naked man who has a tire around him: "I'm fucking despair!"

■▪▪

Q: What were the first pornographic words spoken on prime-time nationwide television?

A: "Ward, don't you think you were a little hard on the Beaver last night?"

■▪▪

A farmer has three daughters of whom he is extremely protective. One evening they all have dates, and so the farmer sits out on the front porch with his shotgun, waiting for the suitors to arrive. The first guy shows up and says, "Hi, my name is Joe. I'm here to see Flo to take her to a show. Is she ready to go?"

The farmer says, "Yeah, she's inside. Go on in."

The second guy comes up the front porch steps and says, "Hi, my name is Eddy. I'm here to see Betty to take her for spaghetti. Is she ready?"

The farmer says, "Yeah, yeah, yeah. Go ahead in the house."

The next guy comes up and says, "Hi, my name is Chuck," and the farmer shoots him.

Q: How do you eat a frog?
A: One leg over each ear.

A man rents a cabin in the woods so that he can go bear hunting. On his first morning out with his rifle, he is in the middle of the forest and is about to come upon a clearing, when he hears a rustling sound. He quickly ducks back behind a tree and slowly peers around the trunk. Lumbering into the clearing is the biggest, meanest-looking grizzly bear the man has ever seen. He slowly lifts his rifle to his shoulder and gets the bear dead center in his sight. He pulls the trigger. POW!

The man runs into the big cloud of smoke in the clearing to get the carcass, but when the smoke clears, there is nothing there. Suddenly, the man feels a tap on his shoulder. He turns around, and there is the immense bear standing over him. The bear pulls the rifle out of the man's hands and then snaps it in half over his furry knee.

The bear says, "I'm tired of all you jerks coming out here and shooting at me all the time. I'm going to teach you a lesson. Turn around, drop your pants, and bend over. NOW!" The terrified, quaking man does just as the bear orders, and the bear proceeds to fuck the man up the ass.

The man goes back to the cabin, and he is incensed. "I'm gonna fix that bear," he mutters to himself. He then drives to the nearest town and buys a bigger rifle.

The next morning, the man goes into the forest in search of the bear. Finally he sees the animal, draws a bead on him, and then fires. BLAM! He runs over to the cloud of smoke where the bear's dead body should be, but when the smoke clears, there's no bear there.

Once again, the man feels a tap on his shoulder. He whips around, and the huge bear rips the gun out of the man's hands and twists the barrel into a pretzel with his huge bare hands. "You people never learn, do you?" says the grizzly. "All right, you know the routine. Bend over and spread 'em." The trembling man does as he is told, and the bear gives it to him again, even worse than the first time.

Now the man is furious with rage. He runs back to the cabin, gets in his truck, drives to town, and buys an elephant gun. As he's driving back to the cabin, the man keeps swearing over and over to himself, "*This* time I'm gonna get him! *This* time I'm gonna get him!"

The next morning, bright and early, the man goes out into the woods in search of the grizzly. He searches all day, and finally, around dusk, he sees the bear drinking from the river. The man takes careful aim with the huge rifle and pulls off the round. BOOM! The kickback of the elephant gun is so strong that it knocks him over, but the man jumps to his feet and runs to the cloud of smoke by the riverside. When it clears, though, there is no bear.

Sure enough, the man feels a tap on his shoulder. When he turns around, the bear looks down at him and says, "Let's be honest. You're not really in this for the *hunting*, are you?"

▰▰▰

Q: What is the speed limit for a woman having sex?
A: Sixty-eight, because at 69 she blows a rod.

▰▰▰

Two retired Jewish men meet while they are vacationing in Florida. One of the men, Murray, is from Georgia and the other man, Irving, is from New York. At the end of their two-week stay in the Sunshine State, Murray says to his new friend, "Irving, in just these two weeks I feel like I've known you all my life. Before you go back to New York, why don't you extend your vacation for a few days and come visit me in Georgia? After all, you're retired, and there's nothing urgent calling you back home. I have a big mansion, a live-in cook, and you can come to see my town and the kind of life I lead. What do you say?"

Irving replies, "That sounds like a great idea."

The two men travel together to Georgia. They spend two days together enjoying life on the large estate. The cook provides them with wonderful meals, and Irving enjoys sleeping in the beautiful guest room with the four-poster bed and antique furniture.

After spending the second night in the luxurious domicile, Irving has a wonderfully cooked gourmet breakfast with his friend. After breakfast, Murray leans over and hands Irving a piece of paper.

Irving looks at the paper, and it is an itemized bill for his stay at the mansion. "Murray," he says, "what is this? It says here that you're charging me for all the food prepared for me by your chef, and that there's even a room fee for each night that I slept here. What's going on?"

"That's correct," Murray replies. "That's your bill for your stay up to now."

Irving is dumbfounded. "You can't be serious," he implores.

Murray is unwavering. "You ate the food and slept in the room, didn't you?"

"Yes, I did," answers Irving, "but you invited me. I thought I was your guest!"

Murray says, "You are my guest, but you still have to pay."

"That's ridiculous!" exclaims Irving. "I'm not paying."

Murray says, "Why don't we go to my rabbi and let him settle this?"

"That's an excellent idea," answers Irving. "Let's go see your rabbi."

The two men go to Murray's town rabbi and Irving explains the situation to him. When Irving is finished, the rabbi says to him, "Okay. Let me see if I have this straight. Murray invited you to be a guest in his home, and then, after two nights, he presented you with a bill. Is that correct?"

"That's it exactly," replies Irving.

"But," asks the rabbi, "did you actually eat the food and sleep in the bed?"

"Yes," says Irving.

The rabbi looks Irving straight in the eye and says, "Then there's no question about it. You have to pay."

Irving is dumbfounded. He and Murray walk out of the rabbi's office and get into Murray's limo. Once inside, Irving gets out his checkbook and writes out a check for the entire amount. With a scowl, he hands the check to Murray. Murray immediately takes the check and rips it up. Now Irving is completely flabbergasted. "What is going on?" he asks. "Why did you make me go through all that?"

"How else," says Murray, "could I show you what a stupid rabbi we have?"

▼▼▼

Q: Why did the feminist cross the road?
A: To SUCK MY DICK!

■▼■

Q: How many feminists does it take to change a lightbulb?
A: Two. One to change the bulb, and the other to SUCK MY DICK!

■▼■

Three inmates from the asylum are up for review to be released. When the first one comes before the board, a member of the panel asks him, "Do you think that you're well enough to be released?"

"Yes, I do," replies the inmate.

The board member then says to him, "All right, answer this question for me. How much is three times three?"

The inmate sinks deep into thought, but suddenly brightens. "*I* know!" he exclaims. "Three times three is *Tuesday*!"

The panel members look at each other and roll their eyes as the man is ushered out of the office and back to his room. A few minutes later, the next inmate is brought in. The head of the panel asks him, "Do you think that you are now ready to leave the institution?"

"Oh yes," answers the inmate.

So the panel member says to him, "Well, then, what is three times three?"

The man thinks for just a moment, then declares triumphantly, "One hundred eighty-one!"

After he is led out, the third inmate is brought before the board. The panel member asks him, "Do you feel that you are ready to cope with the outside world?"

The inmate is very sure of himself as he answers, "Yes, I most certainly am!"

The board member then says, "Very good. Now tell me, what is three times three?"

Without a moment's hesitation, the inmate replies, "Nine."

"Very good!" exclaims the head of the review committee. "How did you arrive at that number?"

"It was simple," replies the inmate. "All I had to do was subtract Tuesday from 181."

■▼■▼

Q: What's the difference between a vitamin and a hormone?
A: You can't make a vitamin.

■▼■▼

A farmer goes to the doctor because he has been having a problem with his sexuality. "Doc," he says, "I'm embarrassed to admit it, but lately I've been having a hard time getting it up."

"Oh," says the doctor, "that's no problem. I can

give you some pills that will clear that up immediately." The doctor goes over to a drawer and pulls out a small container of little purple pills. He hands the vial to the farmer and says sternly, "I just have one warning for you: Take only ONE pill a week. Under *no* circumstance should you ever take any more than that."

The farmer goes home, and before he takes a pill, he decides to try it out first on his stud horse. The horse swallows the pill, immediately jumps over the fence to the corral, runs over to the barn, kicks down one of the barn doors, and gallops off down the road.

The farmer thinks to himself, "These pills are way too strong for me." He goes over to the well and dumps the rest of the pills down the shaft.

A few days later, while doing some errands in town, the farmer happens to run into the doctor. The doctor asks the farmer how well the pills have been working.

"To tell you the truth, Doc," answers the farmer, "I got scared and threw the pills down the well."

"Oh my goodness!" cries the doctor. "You haven't drunk any of the water, have you?"

"No," says the farmer, "we can't get the pump handle down."

▼▼▼

Q: What do a banjo and an artillery shell have in common?

A: With each one, by the time you hear it, it's too late to run.

A man is driving down the road in his brand-new car. This car has all the extras, including a voice-activated radio. All the man has to do is to say the genre out loud, and the radio will change the station automatically. The man is driving along, and to test it out, he says, "Classical!" He quickly hears the radio start playing a beautiful Brahms concerto. The strings are sounding incredibly lush, romantic, and beautiful. The man feels the music so much that he starts to hum along with the radio.

After ten minutes of this, the man says, "Country!" The radio instantly changes the channel to a station that is playing Garth Brooks. The man is really happy to hear the country sound, with the pedal steel guitar twanging in the background. He starts enjoying it so much that he starts to sing along in a loud voice.

Suddenly, from out of nowhere, a car swerves wildly over in front of the man's new car, cutting him off and almost running him off the road. The man yells out, "STUPID JERK!" and the radio station immediately changes to Rush Limbaugh.

Or, depending on your audience . . . to Howard Stern.

▼▼▼

Q: What do you get when you cross an elephant and a skin doctor?
A: A pachydermatologist.

▼▼▼

One fine Sunday evening a priest, a minister, and a rabbi are celebrating the end of their workweek together with a little aperitif. Suddenly, a fly lands right in the priest's glass with a little splash. Carefully, the priest fishes the fly out, shakes it dry, throws it into the air, and says, "Be on your way, little fly."

Only a few moments later, the fly returns and heads straight for the minister's glass. After it splashes into his drink, the minister retrieves the little insect from his beverage and, shaking it off, tosses it into the air, saying, "Be free, little creature."

However, the fly doesn't seem to get the message and just one minute later nose-dives directly into the rabbi's glass. The rabbi grabs the fly and begins to shake it violently, shouting, "Spit it out! Spit it out!"

Q: What do you call a bouncer in a gay bar?
A: A flamethrower.

Three men are on the final day of their training to become FBI agents. They are sitting in an office together when the first man's name is called and he is ushered into a small room. The man behind the desk says, "Congratulations. You have successfully completed your training to become an FBI agent, and we now have one final test of your loyalty. Are you ready?"

The first man answers, "Yes."

The tester then tells him, "We have brought your wife in, and she is in one of the rooms adjoining this one. Here is a gun. You must now go into the next room and kill your wife."

The tester starts to hand the gun to the man, but the guy knocks it away. "Are you crazy or something?" he screams. "I've been married for three years! I love my wife! No job is that important to me! I'm leaving!" he shouts, and storms out of the room.

The second man is then brought in. The tester explains the same thing to him, "Congratulations," he says. "You have successfully completed your training to become an agent, and we now have one final test of your loyalty. Are you ready?"

The second man answers, "I'm ready."

I was telling this joke to a friend, and when I got to this point in the joke, he interrupted me and said, "That poor second guy. He's in every joke, and he never gets to do anything. He's always just repeating the same thing that the first guy did, with maybe a slight variation, and then he's gone. He never gets to do anything original and never gets the laugh. I really feel sorry for that poor second guy."

So I would like to hereby suggest that we all pause for a moment and give a little mental "Thank you" to all those second guys (and occasionally women) who do such an important, yet thankless, job. We must remember that without them, we would not have that wonderful rhythm that is so essential to the payoff of our jokes. So I hereby (and I hope you join me) give my heartfelt gratitude to those tireless guardians of the all-important "Three Rule" in joke telling. THANK YOU, "SECOND GUYS," WHEREVER YOU ARE!

The tester then tells the second guy, "We have brought your wife in, and she is in one of the rooms adjoining this one. Here is a gun. You must now go into the next room and kill your wife."

The tester starts to hand the gun to the man, but the guy refuses to take it. He just shakes his head and says, "I couldn't possibly do that. I have been married for five years and I truly love my wife."

The tester tells the man, "I'm sorry, but you have failed the test. You are not suitable to be an agent for the FBI. Good-bye."

The second man doesn't say a word. He just turns around in disgust and leaves.

They bring the third man into the room, and the tester tells him the same thing. "Your wife is in the next room, and you must take this gun and go in there and kill her."

Without a word, the third man takes the gun and walks into the next room, closing the door behind him. After a few moments of silence, the tester hears a big commotion going on behind the door, with furniture being thrown around and loud thumps on the wall. After about five minutes the sounds stop, all is quiet, and the man walks back into the tester's room. His clothes are all torn, and he is dripping with sweat.

"What happened?" asks the tester.

"Some idiot put *blanks* in the gun," replies the third guy, "and I had to *strangle* her!"

Q: Why do blondes like cars with sunroofs?
A: More legroom.

A man goes into a little neighborhood pub, and when he sits down, he notices a beautiful woman sitting at the other end of the bar. He waves to her, and much to his surprise, she winks back at him. It doesn't take long before he is on the stool next to her.

They talk for about fifteen minutes and then the man says to the woman, "You're really hot!"

"You're pretty cute, too," she says to him. "I'll tell you what. I live just around the corner. What do you think about coming up to my place?"

"It sounds great!" the man eagerly replies.

"Before we go up there, though," the woman says, "I have to ask you one question. Do you like doing it Greek style?"

"Well . . . uh . . . I'm not exactly sure what that is," the man answers, "but it sure sounds interesting and I'm willing to learn! Let's go!"

So the two of them walk over to her apartment. As soon as they get inside the door, the woman rips off all her clothes. The man can't believe his eyes. The woman has an incredibly beautiful body. "Now, you're *sure*," the woman asks, "that you want to do it Greek style?"

"Definitely!" the man replies.

"All right, then," says the woman. "Take off all your clothes, and get up on the bed on your hands and knees."

"Sounds like fun!" the man exclaims. He leaps out of his clothes and climbs onto the bed on his hands and knees.

The woman goes around and gets onto the bed right in front of the man. She kneels down in front of his head. She asks him again, "Are you *sure* that you want to do it Greek style?"

"Yeah! Yeah!" says the man.

The woman grabs the man with her arms right under his armpits, getting him in a lock hold. He can't move at all, and his head is pressing right into her chest.

One more time she says, "Are you *sure* that you want to do it Greek style?"

The man's muffled voice can barely be heard from between her breasts. "Yeah!" he mumbles, "Greek style!"

The woman's grip on him tightens like a vise, and she yells out, "GUS!"

Q: If you're an American when you go into the bathroom, and an American when you come out, what are you when you're *in* the bathroom?
A: European.

A beautiful woman is sitting on a train with an empty seat next to her. A cowboy dressed in a Stetson hat and fancy boots saunters over and says, "Pardon me, ma'am, do you mind if I sit here?"

The woman looks up at him and says, "I most certainly do! Cowboys are disgusting! I hate cowboys! Cowboys are mean, crude, vile, and uncouth! I'll tell you something else I know about cowboys. Cowboys will screw *anything*! Cowboys will fuck sheep, they'll fuck cattle, they'll fuck dogs, they'll fuck lizards, they'll fuck chickens—"

Suddenly the incredulous cowboy asks, "*Chickens?*"

A little boy runs up to his mother and shouts, "Mommy! Mommy! I want to be a drummer when I grow up!"

The mother sweetly replies, "You can't do *both*."

An obscene caller dials a number and a little girl answers. "Hello," she says, ever so politely.

The obscene caller, in his sleaziest-sounding voice, says, "Can I speak to your mother?"

The little girl sweetly replies, "She's not here."

"Oh," growls the caller. "Well, is your sister there?"

"No," the girl answers nicely.

"Then can I talk to the baby-sitter?" he rasps.

The little girl tells him, "She's in the bathroom."

The caller says, in his scratchy voice, "Well, then, how old are you?"

The girl replies, "Five."

"Oh . . . ," says the caller, deep in thought. Then he snarls, "Doo-doo . . . cah-cah . . . pee-pee . . ."

Q: What do you call a dog with metal balls and no hind legs?
A: Sparky.

A boy is taken from his home because of physical abuse. After being in the orphanage for a few weeks, he tells a social worker that he wants to leave. The social worker asks him, "Well, do you want to go back and live with your father again?"

"No," replies the boy. "He beats me."

The social worker says, "Do you want to live with your mother?"

The boy says, "No, she beats me too."

"Well, then," asks the social worker, "who do you want to live with?"

The boy answers, "The New Orleans Saints."

The social worker is taken aback. "The Saints? Why do you want to live with the New Orleans Saints?"

"Because," replies the boy, "they don't beat *any-body*."

God forbid that this book should fall into the hands of any young children. However, kids like jokes, too, so here are some jokes that you can read or tell to your youthful circle of friends.

Q: Why did the chicken cross the playground?
A: To get to the other slide.

Q: What do you have when you've got fifty female pigs and fifty male deer?
A: A hundred sows and bucks.

Q: Why was 6 afraid of 7?
A: Because 7 8 9.

Q: What did the grape do when the elephant sat on it?
A: Let out a little wine.

Q: What do you get when you cross a centipede with a turkey?
A: Drumsticks for *everybody*!

Q: What was the Pilgrims' favorite kind of music?
A: Plymouth rock.

■▄▖

Q: Why do radio announcers have small hands?
A: "Wee paws for station identification."

■▄▖

Q: What time is it when you go to the dentist?
A: Two-thirty.

■▄▖

Two little boys are out playing in a field one day, when they come upon a black hole in the ground. In order to find out how deep it is, they throw a quarter into the hole. They wait and wait, but they don't hear the quarter hit bottom.

They decide to try something larger, so they take a big stone and push it into the hole. They wait again, but they still don't hear any sound, so they decide that they must find something really large.

They look around and they see a large wooden post sticking out of the ground. The two boys go over and they pull and pull, and they finally manage to get it out of the ground. They roll the post over to the hole and push it in. As they are waiting for a sound, they see a goat running like crazy toward the hole, and then the goat jumps right in.

The boys are amazed, and as they stand there waiting for the sound of something to hit the bottom, a farmer walks up to them. "Have you boys seen my goat?" he asks them.

One of the boys says, "Yes, sir. Your goat just ran up to this hole and jumped in."

"That couldn't have been *my* goat," replies the farmer. "My goat was tied to a big wooden post."

This next joke will make it readily apparent to you that we are now out of the children's section of jokes.

Sharon Stone is on a cruise ship when, out of nowhere, a tropical storm hits the boat with its full force. In the ensuing storm, the ship is completely destroyed. Sharon gets washed up on the shore of a nearby deserted island, and when she looks back out to sea, she sees one other survivor from the ship coming toward the island. It is a man, and he has managed to hang on to his suitcase, which he is using as a flotation device. When he reaches the beach, they are both really happy to see another person alive, but darkness is about to fall, so they set about gathering wood for a fire and start searching for some food.

After a few weeks of living together on the island, one moonlit evening the man says to her, "You know,

Sharon, we're alone on this island. Who knows how long we'll be here? I'm a man and you're a woman. Why don't we get to know each other physically?"

Sharon immediately replies, "No way!"

The man just shrugs his shoulders and goes off to look for some firewood for the night.

Three more weeks go by, and by now Ms. Stone is beginning to have second thoughts. "He's actually pretty good looking," she thinks to herself, and so she calls the man over. "Okay," she says, "I'll sleep with you on one condition. You must promise me that after we get rescued, you will *never, ever* tell anyone about this *as long as you live.*"

The man makes a cross over his heart. "I promise," he says.

So they proceed to make love, and the man turns out to be a fantastic lover. They continue to live on the island and are having sex several times a day. After about two weeks, the man says to Sharon, "Would you do me a favor?"

"Sure," she replies.

The man goes over to his suitcase and pulls out a suit, a shirt, and a tie. He says to Sharon, "Could you put these on?"

She looks at him quizzically and says, "Well, it's a little kinky, but all right. I'll do it."

After she puts the suit on and gets the tie on straight, the man asks, "Now, could you go over to the water, wet down your hair, and then slick it back so that it looks really short?"

Sharon agrees to do this, and when she comes

back, the man gets out a little eyebrow pencil. He proceeds to paint a little mustache on Sharon's upper lip. He then says to her, "Could we go for a walk on the beach together?"

"This is getting pretty kinky," she replies, "but okay."

"Now, before we start walking," the man says to her, "I have one final request. Would you mind if I called you Pete?"

"At this point," she answers, "what the hell? Go ahead."

The two of them start to take a nice, leisurely stroll down the beach. After about ten minutes, the man suddenly turns to her and exclaims excitedly, "Pete! Guess what? *I'm fucking Sharon Stone!*"

❖❖❖

Q: What do you call a day that follows two days of rain?
A: Monday.

❖❖❖

The head of the largest organized-crime family in New York is finally arrested and convicted. He is sent to a maximum-security federal penitentiary in the South, where he will be very closely watched for many years to come.

On his first day in prison, during the admission and orientation program, the crime boss is exercising in the rec yard, when a short, bald prisoner walks up to him. "Oh my word," gasps the small inmate. "It's you! The Don of Dons! The undisputed head of the 'Family.' The king of the 'good fellas'! It's such an honor to have you here with us!"

The little man continues, "On behalf of all the inmates here, let me welcome you to our institution. I know that it's not so great to be in prison, but I must tell you that if you have to be in a correctional facility, then *this* is the one to be in. Just to show you what I mean, let me tell you about some of our activities here at 'Club Fed.'

"Every Monday night we have 'Sports Night.' We have softball, basketball, touch football, and tennis leagues. Each season we have tournaments with playoff games, and at the end of the season, we have a big awards ceremony with trophies and everything. You're gonna *love* Monday nights!

"On Tuesday nights we have 'Talent Night.' We have a prison band, and every Tuesday night we put on a show. Sometimes it's a prison comedian, sometimes it is a musical, and sometimes we put on dramatic plays. At the end of the year, we have a big awards dinner and give out trophies for outstanding achievement. You're gonna *love* Tuesday nights!

"Now, on Wednesday nights— Oh by the way, Godfather, are you gay?" asks the little man.

"No," replies the underworld boss.

"Ooooh," the little man winces, "I don't think you're gonna *like* Wednesday nights."

I was trading jokes with one of my passengers one night and I asked him if he wanted to hear a sexist joke that I had just heard. He said, "Okay."

So I said, "Yeah, but this is just about the most sexist joke I've ever heard."

"Better still," said the man. So I told him this joke:

Q: Why don't women's vaginas fall off?

A: Because the vacuum in their brain creates a natural suction.

After I told the punch line there was a dead silence. Then the man said, "I like it." There was another pause and then he said, "A lot."

We drove on a little farther, and then I asked the man, "What kind of work do you do?"

He replied, "I am a gynecologist."

Q: Why is it that only women should get hemorrhoids?

A: Because when God created man, He created the perfect asshole.

Two executives working in the garment center are having lunch together. Goldstein says to his friend, "Last week was one of the worst weeks of my entire life."

"What happened?" asks Birnbaum.

Goldstein moans, "My wife and I went to Florida on vacation. It rained for seven days and seven nights, so my wife went out and spent thousands of dollars on the credit card. I came back to New York and found out that my rat brother-in-law accountant has been ripping me off for millions. And to top it all off, when I came in to work on Monday morning, I found my son *shtupping* my best model on my desk!"

"You think *you* had a bad week?" responds Birnbaum. "My week was even worse! I went to Florida on vacation with my wife and it rained for seven days and seven nights, so my wife went out and spent thousands on the credit card. Then, when I got back to New York, I found out that my rat cousin accountant has been ripping me off for millions. To top it all off, when I came in to my office on Monday, I found my son *shtupping* my best model on my desk!"

"How can you say that your week was worse than mine?" asks Goldstein. "It was identical!"

"Shmuck!" replies Birnbaum. "I manufacture *men's* wear!"

Q: How many mice does it take to screw in a light-bulb?

A: Two. The trick is getting them in there.

A priest and a rabbi who are very good friends coincidentally need to buy new cars at the same time, so they decide to go shopping together. They visit all the automobile dealers, and both of them wind up choosing to buy the same model and same make of car.

They buy the two automobiles and are just about to drive them out of the dealership, when the priest says to his friend, "I have an idea. Wouldn't it be a nice gesture for each of us to bless the other one's car?"

"That's a great idea," replies the rabbi.

So the priest goes over to the rabbi's car and sprinkles it with holy water. Then the rabbi goes over to the priest's car and cuts an inch off the tail pipe.

Q: How can a pregnant woman tell that she's carrying a future lawyer?
A: She has an uncontrollable craving for baloney.

Princess Margaret is about to be a guest contestant on a game show. The show is one in which the picture of an object is projected onto a screen. The audience sees the picture, then the contestant asks questions that can be answered with "yes" or "no," and tries to guess what the object is.

Princess Margaret is waiting in the wings as the

show begins with a lively musical fanfare. The announcer of the show bounds out onto the stage and welcomes the audience to the studio. He then introduces the special guest contestant, and Princess Margaret walks out onto the stage to enthusiastic applause and takes her seat.

The host, in his typical announcer/M.C. voice, says, "Ladies and gentlemen, we are now going to show you the object on the screen. Viewers at home will see it on your television sets, and you folks in the studio audience will see it on the monitors. Princess Margaret will, of course, be unable to see the object from where she is sitting. Now! Ladies and gentlemen! Here is the object!"

On the screen is projected the image of a horse's cock.

The announcer says, "Now, ladies and gentlemen, you have seen the object! Princess Margaret, what is your first question?"

Princess Margaret thinks for a moment, and then asks, "Is it edible?"

A few people in the audience start to titter with laughter, and the host answers, "Well . . . yeee- . . . well . . . nnn- . . . well, *maybe*."

Princess Margaret then says, "Is it a horse's cock?"

▼▼▼

Q: What do you call a lesbian with fat fingers?
A: Well hung.

A woman goes into a sex shop and, after looking around for a while, asks the man behind the counter, "How much are the dildos?" The clerk reaches into the display case and pulls out a box. He takes the dildo out of the box and stands it up on the glass countertop. "This white dildo here is fifteen dollars," he says.

The woman looks at it for a moment, and then asks, "What else do you have?"

The man reaches into the case again and pulls out another box. "This *black* dildo here," he says, "is twenty-five dollars." He takes the black dildo out of the box and stands it on the counter.

The woman picks up each dildo, feels it for a moment, and then asks, "How much is that plaid dildo over there on that shelf behind you?"

The clerk turns around and looks at the shelf behind him. "Oh, that's an expensive one," he says. "That one costs seventy-five dollars."

"Hmm," the woman says, thinking it over. "You know what? I'm going to take the plaid one." She pays the man the seventy-five dollars and leaves.

A few minutes later, the owner of the store comes in and notices the two dildos standing on the counter. He says, "Have you been selling some dildos today?"

"Yes, I have," replies the clerk.

"How many have you managed to move?" asks the owner.

The clerk answers, "Well, I sold five *white* dildos at fifteen dollars apiece, I sold seven *black* dildos at twenty-five dollars apiece, and I managed to get seventy-five dollars for your thermos!"

Q: Why do blondes wear underwear?
A: To keep their ankles warm.

A millionaire decides that he wants to get married, but he wants to marry a virgin. One is not so easy to find in this day and age, but he starts scouring the country in search of his virgin. After a few months of looking, the millionaire is out on a date one night, and he thinks he may have finally found his honey.

The woman seems extremely innocent, so after dinner, as they're riding in the back of his limousine, the man whips out his cock. "Oh my goodness!" exclaims the woman. "What in the world is *that*?"

"You don't know what this is?" asks the millionaire.

"Oh, no!" replies the woman. "I've never seen anything like that in my *whole life*!"

The man puts his dick away, reaches over, and starts hugging the woman. "I love you!" he cries. "I'm going to marry you! I'm going to make you the richest, happiest woman in the whole world!"

A month later they get married. On their wedding night in the hotel room, the husband sits down on the bed next to his wife. He pulls out his penis and says to her, "Are you sure you've never seen anything like this?"

"Never," says the woman, her eyes wide with wonder.

"Well," explains the man, "this is my *cock*."

"No, it's not!" says the woman, in total disbelief.

"It's not?" asks the puzzled millionaire.

"No," answers the wife. "Cocks are *twelve inches* and *black*!"

Q: What kind of meat do priests eat?
A: Nun.

One guy tells his friend, "Guess what? I took a skydiving lesson."

"Gee, that's great!" says the friend. "When did you do that?"

The guy replies, "I had my first lesson last Friday."

"How did it go?"

"Well, it wasn't bad," says the first guy. "There were three of us in the course. The instructor gave us a class on how to jump, and then they took us up in a plane. When we got up to an altitude of a thousand feet, the instructor turned to one of the students and said, 'O.K. You're going first.'

"The student said, 'I can't. I'm really scared!'

"The instructor told him, 'Look, if you don't jump, I'm going to push you.' So the guy jumped.

"Then the instructor said to the other student, 'Now it's your turn.'

"But the student said, 'I can't. We're up too high. I'm scared!'

"Once again, the instructor said, 'If you don't jump, I'm going to push you.'

"So the second guy jumped. Then the instructor turned to me. 'It's your turn to jump,' he said.

"By now, though, I was terrified. I said to him, 'I can't! I'm really scared!'

"The instructor told me, 'Buddy, if you don't jump, I'm going to push you.'

"But I said, 'I can't! I can't! I'm petrified!'

"Then the instructor shouted at me, 'IF YOU

DON'T JUMP, I'M GOING TO FUCK YOU UP
THE ASS!'"

"Wow!" exclaims the friend hearing this story.
"Did you jump?"

The guy says, "Yeah, a little at first."

■▀■

Q: What's the first thing a blonde does in the morning?
A: Puts her clothes on and goes home.

■▀■

A man is on his way out to play golf on a Saturday morning when his wife says to him, "Please,
honey! I need for you to come home and help me
prepare for the party tonight. Please don't play all
eighteen holes. Just play nine holes, and then come
home. All right? Please?"

The man promises to play just nine holes and
then come right home. He then goes out to the golf
course, meets his friends, and they start to play. After
the ninth hole he turns to his buddies and says,
"Look, you guys. My wife is having a big party
tonight and I've got to go home and help her out.
I'm sorry, but I really have to leave right now."

The friends grumble a little bit, but the man, true
to his word, gets into his car and starts the drive
home. As he's on the highway, he sees a woman broken down on the side of the road. She looks pretty
helpless and scared, so the man pulls over to help.

He gets out and sees that the problem is a flat tire. "Would you like me to fix that for you?" he asks.

"Could you, please?" says the woman. "I don't know anything about this stuff."

So the man gets the jack out of her trunk and quickly changes the tire for her. When he's done, he says to the woman, "Well, I've got to hurry home now."

The woman says, "Listen. You're all hot and sweaty. Why don't you come over to my place, take a shower, and get freshened up? I live right by the next exit."

The man thinks for a moment and then decides. "All right, I will," he says. "Thank you."

He gets back in his car and follows the woman as she drives back to her apartment. When they get there he takes a shower, and as he's drying off, the woman comes into the room, completely naked. "You were so nice to help me out that I want to thank you by taking you into my bedroom right now." They go into her room, and she makes passionate love to him for about three hours.

Afterward, the man drives home, and as he's pulling into his driveway, he sees his wife standing by the kitchen door, arms folded and tapping her foot. "So . . . ?" she says, murder in her eyes.

"Honey," the man starts out, "I can't lie to you. I only played nine holes, but as I was driving home I saw a woman by the side of the road with a flat tire, so I stopped and helped her change it. She was so thankful that she suggested I come over to her place and get cleaned up, and since I was coming home to you, I didn't want to be all hot and sweaty, so I went over there and took a shower. When I came out of the shower, though, the woman was standing there naked, and said she wanted to thank me by making love to me, so we made wild love for about three hours."

The wife looks at the man and screams, "You bastard! I knew it! You played *eighteen holes!*"

Q: What has four legs, is big, green, furry, and if it fell out of a tree it would kill you?
A: A pool table.

A man goes into a bar, and he sees the fine figure of a woman sitting down at the other end. She starts giving the man the eye. He notices that she is wearing a beautiful necklace, and some stunning diamond rings on her long fingers. The man goes over and starts talking to her, and it becomes immediately apparent that they are talking about the same thing. She says to him, "Do you like hand jobs?"

The man smiles and says, "Yeah!"

So she says, "Well, I happen to give the best hand jobs in the business. Five hundred dollars."

"Five hundred dollars for a hand job?" the man exclaims.

"Do you see this necklace and all this jewelry on

my hands?" she says. "I bought all of this *only* with money I made giving hand jobs."

By this time, the man has had a few drinks and he has some money in his pocket, so he says, "All right. Let's go."

They go out to the alley behind the bar and the man gets the most incredible hand job of his life. When they get back inside the bar, the man pays her and says, "I've got to admit, that was the best hand job I've ever had. It was worth every penny! I can't believe it!"

Then she asks him, "Do you like blow jobs?"

The man replies, "Of course! How much?"

"A thousand."

"What?" cries the man. "A thousand dollars for a blow job?"

"Come over here," she says, and leads him to the front window. She draws the curtain aside and points out. "Do you see that Rolls Royce out there?" she asks.

"Uh-huh," says the man.

"I bought that, and two others exactly like it, *just* with money I made by giving blow jobs. I'm the *best* in the business."

The man thinks for a moment, and then says, "Well, the hand job was worth the money. Okay! Let's do it!"

Once again they go out into the back alley, and the man receives the best blow job in his entire life. They go back inside the bar, and the man gives her the thousand.

"That was truly amazing!" he exclaims. "I had no idea that a blow job could be so good! But you know," he says, lowering his voice and leaning in a little closer, "what I'm *really* interested in is some *pussy*."

"Let me show you something," she says, and leads him back over to the front window. She pulls the curtain open and points out to a tall building. "Do you see that big high-rise building over there?" she asks the man.

"Yes," he replies.

She says, "If I had a pussy, I'd *own* one of those."

■▼■

A Jewish man boards a commercial airliner, and when he gets to his assigned seat, he finds that he has been put right next to two Arabs. The Jewish man has the aisle seat, and the Arabs are sitting in the two inside seats. The Jewish man greets the Arabs amiably, sits down, immediately takes off his shoes, and puts his feet up. He has just gotten comfortable and is about to drift off to sleep, when the Arab next to the window stands up.

"Excuse me," says the Arab, "but I'd like to go and get myself a Coke."

The Jewish man sits up and replies, "Hey, I'd be glad to get you a Coke. Just sit back down, relax, and I'll have your Coke for you in a minute."

He stands up and walks down the aisle to get the soda. While he is away, the Arab looks down and notices that the Jewish man has left his shoes on the floor. The Arab leans over and spits into one of the shoes.

A moment later the Jewish man returns. "Here is your Coke," he says kindly, handing it to the Arab. "I hope that you enjoy it."

The Jewish man sits down, puts his feet up, and has just gotten comfortable again when the Arab in the middle stands up. "Excuse me," says the second Arab, "but that Coke looked so good that I just *have* to get one for myself."

"Hey," says the Jewish guy, "I'll be glad to get one for you, too. Sit there, relax, and I'll be right back." With a smile, he goes off to get the other Arab his Coke.

This time, the second Arab leans down and spits into the man's other shoe. When the Jewish man returns, he gives the second Arab his Coke. "There you go," he says, "and if you want another, please feel free to ask."

So the Jewish man finally gets to sit down and get comfortable. He puts his feet up and falls contentedly asleep.

A couple hours later, the airplane lands and the three men start getting ready to deplane. The Jewish man puts on his shoes, and as soon as he stands up, he realizes exactly what has happened. He turns to the two Arabs next to him, and in a very exasperated voice says to them, "Oh, my God, when is all this nonsense between us going to *end*? The spitting in the shoes . . . the pissing in the Cokes . . ."

▼▼▼

Q: What has three legs and an asshole right on the top?

A: A drum stool.

Being a drummer I must, of course, take this joke in its most literal sense.

▼▼▼

An old man and old woman are out for a drive, when a motorcycle cop pulls them over. The policeman gets off of his cycle and walks up to the driver's side of the stopped car. When the old man rolls down the window, the cop says to him, "Did you know that you were doing fifty-five in a thirty-five-mile-an-hour zone?"

The old lady leans over to her husband and squawks, "WHAT? WHAT? WHAT DID HE SAY?"

The old man says to the cop, "She's a little hard of hearing," then leans over to his wife and says, "HE SAID THAT WE WERE DOING FIFTY-FIVE IN A THIRTY-FIVE-MILE-AN-HOUR ZONE."

The cop then asks the man, "May I see your license and registration?"

The old lady leans over and screams in her husband's ear, "WHAT? WHAT? WHAT DID HE SAY?"

The old man turns to the old woman and says, "HE SAID THAT HE WANTS TO SEE MY

LICENSE AND REGISTRATION." The old man hands the officer his license and registration.

The policeman looks at the paperwork and says to the man, "I see from your license here that you folks are from Ohio."

The old lady screams, "WHAT? WHAT? WHAT DID HE SAY?"

The old man says to her, "HE SAID THAT HE CAN TELL FROM THE LICENSE THAT WE'RE FROM OHIO."

"You know," the cop says to the old man, "I had the *worst* sexual experience of my *life* in Ohio."

"WHAT?" screeches the old lady. "WHAT? WHAT? WHAT DID HE SAY?"

The old man turns to his wife and replies, "HE SAYS THAT HE THINKS HE *KNOWS* YOU!"

■■■

Did you hear about the dyslexic rabbi? He was walking around everywhere saying, "Yo!"

■■■

Two southern belles are talking, and one of them has just returned from a trip up to New York City. "Do you know," she tells her friend confidentially, "that up there in New York, they have *men* who kiss *men*?"

"Mercy me!" replies the friend. "What do they call people like that?"

"Well," says the traveler, "they call those people

homosexuals. And do you know, up there in New York, they have *women* who kiss *women?"*

"Oh, my Lord," cries the other woman, totally shocked. "What on earth do they call people like *that?"*

"Well," says the first woman, "they call those people *lesbians.* And . . . do you know that up there in New York they have men who kiss women '*down there'?"*

"Heavens to Betsy!" gasps the incredulous friend. "I don't believe it! Why, what on earth do they call people like *that?"*

"Well," says the first woman, "once I regained my composure, I called him '*precious'!"*

■▼■

One September evening in 1988, I was driving east on Thirteenth Street, when I saw a group of people coming out of a restaurant. As I slowed down to see if they would be needing a cab, I saw that one of the men standing there was Christopher Reeve. As I was watching him, he looked up, caught my eye, and hailed me. He then held up one finger, indicating for me to wait one minute.

As I sat in the cab, I saw that Christopher was with another man and two women. The man had his back to me as he put on his coat. He turned around, and as the group of people started walking toward my cab I saw that the other man was Robin Williams.

Robin got into the backseat and sat between the two

women, while Christopher opened the front door and sat down next to me. I couldn't believe my luck! They said that we would be making two stops. Once they had given me their first destination, I started driving and asked them if they had heard any good jokes lately.

Robin asked me the question of a one-liner, and I gave him the punch line. Everyone in the car laughed, and then I asked Robin a one-liner, and he replied with the punch line. We entertained the other people in the cab like this for several minutes (I'm proud to say that I held my own with Robin—neither one of us could stump the other) and then one of us told a Dan Quayle joke.

This set Robin off on a routine about George Bush (it was the day after Bush had gotten the date of Pearl Harbor wrong during a speech to a veterans' group). Robin's main theme was about two veterans in the audience at Bush's speech talking to each other. "September seventh, the day of infamy? Oh yeah, that was that weekend we took that shore leave."

I couldn't possibly try to recount his entire routine here, because it just wouldn't be funny without hearing Robin's rapid-fire delivery, including all the appropriate accents and sound effects. I will tell you, though, that it was as funny as anything I've ever heard him do on television or in a movie. The man is, without a doubt, a comedic improvisational genius.

A little bit later (fortunately, it was a fairly long fare), there was a momentary lull in Robin's hilarity, and I handed him a copy of my first book. "Check this out," I said. Robin opened it up and started reading jokes out of my book to the other passengers, making them all laugh loudly.

At one point, as Robin was reading the fifth or sixth joke, I looked over at Christopher Reeve laughing and thought to myself, "This is amazing! This has got to be one of my life's peak experiences! I have Popeye in the backseat reading material out of my book, cracking up Superman on the seat next to me!"

Robin then told me a very funny joke that he had heard that was at the expense of a certain bodybuilding comedian. After I stopped laughing at the joke, Robin said, "Don't tell anybody I said that. I can just see the headlines: Man Who Works Out Kills Comedian In Hotel Room!"

After several failed attempts to tell Robin a joke that he hadn't yet heard, I got him with a musician joke that I had heard from one of my teachers at the Berklee College of Music. He laughed enthusiastically, so I finally felt like I had upheld my honor.

When I got them to their first destination, I asked Robin to sign my book for me. He signed it, then he and his lady friend got out of the cab. Chris Reeve went around and got in the backseat to sit with his woman friend, and as I was starting to pull away, I heard Robin shout loudly.

I stopped immediately, thinking that maybe he had forgotten something in the cab. I looked around, but he wasn't even looking in the direction of the taxi. I said to Chris Reeve, "Was he yelling to us?"

"Nah," said Christopher, "he was just working the room."

When we got to the final stop, I asked Mr. Reeve to also sign my book. He did, paid me, then he and his friend left. I opened up the book and saw Christopher Reeve's autograph. Then I looked up at the top of the page and saw that Robin had signed my book, "You give great hack—Robin Williams."

A man having trouble with his sink calls the plumber to his house. After the plumber looks at the pipes, he leans back and tells the man, "I can fix the problem, but before I start, I want you to know that my fee is a hundred and fifty dollars per half hour."

"A hundred and fifty a *half* hour!" says the startled man. "Why, I'm a brain surgeon, and I only get one-fifty for a *full* hour."

"Hey, don't feel bad," says the plumber sympathetically. "When I was a brain surgeon, I didn't get any more than one-fifty an hour, either."

The Post Office stopped production on the new stamp commemorating the American lawyer. People didn't know which side to spit on.

Three engineers are sitting around talking, when the conversation begins to focus on what kind of engineer God was. The first man says, "Well, I think that it's pretty obvious that God was a *mechanical* engineer. All you have to do to prove that is to look at the human body. Think of how the muscles are attached to the bones with ligaments, and how the muscles work as a system of levers and pulleys. This is an unparalleled *masterpiece* of *mechanical* engineering."

The second man replies, "Ah, but I think that God was an *electrical* engineer. After all, what controls the muscles? The brain! With the electrical impulses that the brain sends out, and how it all works with the flashing of the neurons, why, this is a masterpiece of *electrical* engineering!"

The third man replies, "I'm afraid that you're *both* wrong. I think that it's quite obvious that God was a *civil* engineer. Who else would have put a raw sewage-disposal pipeline through a pristine recreational area?"

■▪■

A cabdriver is driving down the street, when suddenly he looks over and sees the Pope frantically waving his arms and yelling, "TAXI! TAXI!" The cabdriver immediately swerves over to the curb and the Pope quickly jumps into the backseat.

"Take me to Kennedy Airport!" he cries. "My limo just broke down and I don't have time to wait for them to fix it! I just *have* to make that last flight to Rome! Hurry!"

"You got it!" replies the cabdriver. He hits the gas and they head uptown on Madison Avenue. Unfortunately, they run into a bit of traffic and have to stop for several red lights.

While they are waiting for the fourth red light to change to green, the Pope is getting more and more anxious. "Hurry! Hurry!" he pleads. "I've just *got* to make this plane!"

"Look, your pontiffship," replies the cabbie. "This *is* rush hour and we've run into some traffic. I'm going as fast as I can. If I run a red light, I'll get a ticket. There's nothing more that I can do!"

At the next light, the Pope becomes extremely agitated. Suddenly he gets an idea. "I'll make you a deal," he says to the cabbie, "let *me* drive!"

"YOU want to drive?" asks the incredulous cab-driver.

"Please!" replies the Pope. "This is the last flight, and I can't miss it! You've *got* to let me drive!"

"How can I say no to you?" says the cabbie. He jumps out and gets into the backseat while the Pope gets out and slides into the front. As soon as he gets behind the wheel, it is 'pedal to the metal' time. With a loud screeching of tires, the Pope swiftly pulls out. He begins screaming sixty miles an hour through the city streets, dodging through traffic, running red lights, and driving up on the sidewalks. He gets on the Grand Central Parkway, and when he hits ninety miles an hour a cop sees the cab fly by.

With the siren blaring and his lights flashing, the cop chases the cab for five miles before the Pope finally pulls over. The police car pulls up behind the stopped cab and the cop jumps out. He walks quickly up to the driver's side of the cab, and the Pope rolls down the window. The policeman looks in and sees him, then nervously says, "Wait right here. Don't go away. I'll be *right* back!"

He runs back to the squad car and calls his sergeant on the radio. "Sarge," he says, "I just pulled this guy over, and I'm not sure whether I should give him a ticket or not. I think he's *really* important."

"Who is it?" asks the sergeant over the radio. "Is it the mayor?"

"No," says the cop, "I think he might be more important than that."

"Is it the governor?" the sergeant asks.

"No," replies the policeman. "I think he might be more important than *that*."

"Did you pull over the *president*?" asks the sergeant.

"No," answers the cop, "but I think this guy might even be more important than THAT!"

"Well," says the sergeant impatiently, "who is it?"

"I don't know," replies the policeman, "but the Pope is his *driver*!"

It's nice to have a joke where the cabdriver is the big shot!

Cabbies, after all, do deserve a lot of respect for doing a tough job. It's very grueling to sit for twelve hours with virtually no breaks, fight all the traffic, and to risk the danger of accidents and robberies.

That's why I'll be eternally grateful to all of you out there who got into my cab and lightened my load with laughter.